A lone ruby ring in a velvet case...

It all began when a young Vittoria Perrone fell madly in love with an American pilot during the Second World War. But their love put sweet Vittoria in danger, so the soldier left, promising to one day claim her as his bride.

Time passed and Vittoria's family pledged her to another, Giovanni Valente. Just before the day that promised to be her darkest—her wedding day—her beloved American, Enrico Covelli, returned, asking for her hand in marriage.

Vittoria pleaded to be released from her marital obligation. Angry, Giovanni took the Perrone family betrothal rings, snatched the bride's band and placed it on his little finger, swearing never to give it up. Forevermore, the Covelli family was to be cursed!

Fifty years later the hex remained...only to be lifted if the heirloom ruby ring [illegible] the name of love and retur[illegible] heir, Vittoria's lovely firstb[illegible] Angelina Covelli.

***This** is Angelina's story...*

Dear Reader,

The end of the century is near, and we're all eagerly anticipating the wonders to come. But no matter what happens, I believe that everyone will continue to need and to seek the unquenchable spirit of love...of *romance*. And here at Silhouette Romance, we're delighted to present another month's worth of terrific, emotional stories.

This month, RITA Award-winning author Marie Ferrarella offers a tender BUNDLES OF JOY tale, in which *The Baby Beneath the Mistletoe* brings together a man who's lost his faith and a woman who challenges him to take a chance at love...and family. In Charlotte Maclay's charming new novel, a millionaire playboy isn't sure what he was *Expecting at Christmas,* but what he gets is a *very* pregnant butler! Elizabeth Harbison launches her wonderful new theme-based miniseries, CINDERELLA BRIDES, with the fairy-tale romance—complete with mistaken identity!—between *Emma and the Earl.*

In *A Diamond for Kate* by Moyra Tarling, discover whether a doctor makes his devoted nurse his devoted wife *after* learning about her past.... Patricia Thayer's cross-line miniseries WITH THESE RINGS returns to Romance and poses the question: Can *The Man, the Ring, the Wedding* end a fifty-year-old curse? You'll have to read this dramatic story to find out! And though *The Millionaire's Proposition* involves making a baby in Natalie Patrick's upbeat Romance, can a down-on-her-luck waitress also convince him to make beautiful memories...as man and wife?

Enjoy this month's offerings, and look forward to a new century of timeless, traditional tales guaranteed to touch your heart!

Mary-Theresa Hussey

Mary-Theresa Hussey
Senior Editor, Silhouette Romance

Please address questions and book requests to:
Silhouette Reader Service
U.S.: 3010 Walden Ave., P.O. Box 1325, Buffalo, NY 14269
Canadian: P.O. Box 609, Fort Erie, Ont. L2A 5X3

THE MAN, THE RING, THE WEDDING

Patricia Thayer

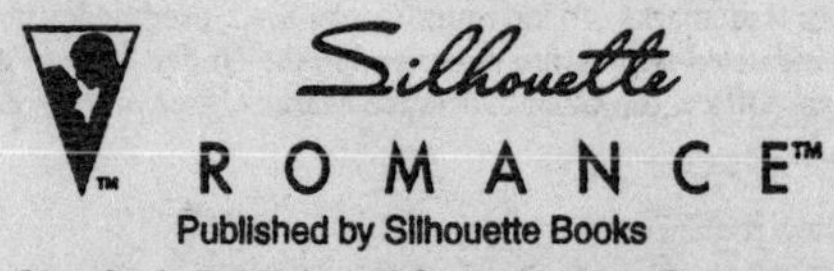

Published by Silhouette Books
America's Publisher of Contemporary Romance

To all the new brides and grooms in my family this year.
Amy and Kelly Klossner, Heather and Chris Beam, and
especially to my son and his wife, Brett and Daralynn.
Here's to a lifetime of love and romance.

To Millie Caggiano—
thanks for sharing your big Italian family with me.

SILHOUETTE BOOKS

ISBN 0-373-19412-9

THE MAN, THE RING, THE WEDDING

This edition published by arrangement with Harlequin Books S.A.

Visit us at www.romance.net

Printed in U.S.A.

Books by Patricia Thayer

Silhouette Romance

Just Maggie #895
Race to the Altar #1009
The Cowboy's Courtship #1064
Wildcat Wedding #1086
Reilly's Bride #1146
The Cowboy's Convenient Bride #1261
**Her Surprise Family* #1394
**The Man, the Ring, the Wedding* #1412

Silhouette Special Edition

Nothing Short of a Miracle #1116
Baby, Our Baby! #1225
**The Secret Millionaire* #1252

*With These Rings

PATRICIA THAYER

has been writing for fourteen years and has published over ten books with Silhouette. Her books have been nominated for the National Readers' Choice Award, Virginia Romance Writers of America's Holt Medallion and a prestigious RITA Award. In 1997, *Nothing Short of a Miracle* won the *Romantic Times Magazine* Reviewers' Choice Award for Best Special Edition.

Thanks to the understanding men in her life—her husband of twenty-eight years, Steve, and her three sons—Pat has been able to fulfill her dream of writing romance. Another dream is to own a cabin in Colorado, where she can spend her days writing and her evenings with her favorite hero, Steve. She loves to hear from readers. You can write to her at P.O. Box 6251, Anaheim, CA 92816-0251.

WISCONSIN
Lake Michigan
MICHIGAN
Chicago
Ft. Wayne
INDIANA
ILLINOIS
Indianapolis
OHIO
Bloomington
Haven Springs
N
Louisville
KENTUCKY
All underlined places are fictitious.

Chapter One

She was looking at her future.

Angelina Covelli walked up the concrete steps of the historic hotel, passing by the familiar brass plaque on the cornerstone that read Grand Haven Hotel 1898. The old stone building had been a landmark in Haven Springs for the past thirty years.

Standing at the weathered oak doors, Angelina traced her fingers over beveled window panels with the initials GH cut into the frosted glass. Then taking a deep breath to renew her courage, she stepped across the threshold and went inside. After waiting for her eyes to adjust to the dimly lit lobby, she glanced around. Dust and cobwebs covered nearly everything, and a musty odor hung in the stuffy air.

Angelina smiled and slowly pivoted in a circle, trying to take in all the grandeur. "Incredible," she breathed, her soft voice echoing off the bare walls.

She had toured the hotel once before with her brothers, but there hadn't been nearly enough time to take everything in. She hoped to be able to see a lot more of this place in the following months when Covelli and Sons secured the bid to renovate. Her excitement—and relief—grew. The family business would be financially stable again. Just like when her dad was alive.

The last two years had been rough ones, but that was about to end along with her job as office manager for the family construction business. She could finally move on with her life—find that niche that would fulfill her and give her independence. But first she had to find the man who was going to help her.

"Hello, is anyone here?" Angelina called out as she approached the dark oak front desk with the intricately carved detail and marble top. Where was he? she wondered. John Rossi's assistant had told her his boss would be arriving today. Although their appointment wasn't until tomorrow afternoon, Angelina didn't want to miss the chance to speak to the CEO before every other contractor descended on the hotel. She was going to make sure she made an impression—and was awarded the renovation job.

Walking along the grimy marble floor, she was careful her heels didn't catch in the cracked tile. Her attention was drawn to the crystal teardrop chandeliers that hung from the high ceiling, making an elegant pathway through the large lobby and ending at a wide staircase that led to the second-floor balcony.

She climbed the steps cushioned by once-scarlet carpeting, now torn and faded by age. What a shame this beautiful place hadn't been taken care of. Running a hand along the brass railing, she made the long trip to the top, wondering what it had been like to spend an evening as a guest here in the hotel's heyday.

Her grandmother Vittoria had told her stories about

the society balls held upstairs in the grand ballroom. Women dressed in long satin gowns and men in tuxedos had come from all around. Angelina hadn't been to a formal dance since her prom. She smiled. She nearly hadn't had a date that night because her brother Rick had threatened to break Jimmy Hitchcock's arm if he got out of line.

No wonder men won't come near me, Angelina thought, then sadly remembered *why* she was alone. It had been her choice, ever since she had lost the wonderful man she had met in college. Within two seconds she'd known that the handsome man with the warm hazel eyes would be her one true love. They were destined to be together…forever. But that had all changed when he died, leaving her alone. Love had betrayed her—now she was concentrating on her career.

She pushed away any sad thoughts as she turned and started back down the steps, imagining herself in an elegant, floor-length dress, a handsome man waiting for her at the front of the sweeping staircase. Someone like… She caught a sudden movement out of the corner of her eye. She jerked her head around to find a man standing in the shadows.

She gasped as her heart nearly jumped into her throat. The tall stranger had dark short hair and piercing eyes. He was dressed in faded jeans, a denim shirt and work boots.

"I'm sorry," she said quickly. "I didn't know anyone was here." Who was he?

"What are you doing here?" he asked, as he approached the bottom step.

"I have an appointment," she lied. "With Mr. Rossi. And you are?"

John Rossi watched as the beautiful woman came

down the stairs. She was small in stature, but her body didn't lack curves. His gaze moved over her charcoal-colored business jacket then lingered on her hips covered by a slim skirt.

"You could say that I work here," he murmured, taking advantage of his angle to study her long, gorgeous legs.

"Oh, so you're getting things ready for Mr. Rossi's arrival?"

Slowly, his eyes raised to meet her sky-blue gaze. "Actually, I am—"

She waved a hand. "I'll be working for Rossi International, too. That's why I'm here."

John stood back as she tossed her long midnight hair off her shoulders, his fingers itching to discover the softness of the silky strands. His body swiftly reacted to this sexy woman. She had flawless olive skin. A small, slender nose. But it was her mouth, her full, rosy lips, that had him distracted. He shook his head, trying to remember why he was here. And why this woman shouldn't be. How did she get past security?

"So you have a job with Rossi?" he said.

That sensual mouth of hers twitched mischievously. "Well, not exactly. But I'm sure by tomorrow that will change."

He folded his arms over his chest and leaned a hip against the brass staircase railing. He knew he should tell her who he was, but this conversation was too interesting to cut short. He cocked an eyebrow. "What is it you do exactly—and are so good at—that you know for sure you'll be hired?"

"Well, I'm good at computers. Excellent, in fact." She shook her head and her eyes widened. "But it's not me. It's my family business, Covelli and Sons. My brothers, Rick and Rafe, are bidding on the renovation job on this hotel.''

John froze, fighting to hide his surprise. So this was Angelina Covelli. They weren't supposed to meet until tomorrow. ''What time is your appointment?''

''Actually I'm a bit early.''

Like twenty-four hours, he thought. ''A little eager?''

''I just don't want to miss an opportunity.'' Angelina finished her trip down the steps and began walking around the lobby. ''I mean, look at this place. It needs a lot of work by expert hands to ensure it doesn't lose its beautiful grandeur. Nothing should be changed, just restored. Like the front desk. Keep it just as is, except for installing computers. My brothers can handle that without any problems,'' she assured him.

John followed her to the desk and watched as she ran her hand over the marble surface. He quickly grabbed her wrist. ''Careful, you'll get dirty.''

His gaze locked again on her incredible eyes. Feeling the heat surge through him, he released her arm. ''This place hasn't been deemed safe yet. It's being checked out today by the building engineer. There could be unsafe areas.''

''Is that your job?''

He was ready to tell her who he was. ''It's one of my jobs, but I'm here because—'' He paused. ''I need to get things ready for tomorrow.''

Her smile dropped. ''I was hoping to meet Mr. Rossi today.''

''I believe he's scheduled all appointments for tomorrow,'' John said.

''But I want to see him first. Pitch my outline of ideas for the renovation, one on one. It's so hard to talk with a roomful of other contractors around.'' Her blue eyes met his and a slow smile spread across her face. ''Maybe you could help me. Put in a good word for me and my company.''

She opened her thin leather briefcase and pulled out a folder. ''We have tons of references. And we've been in business for over thirty years. Please,'' she said, pushing the folder towards him. ''Could you at least give this to him?''

John raised his hands, knowing he had to tell her who he was. ''Look Ms....''

''Covelli, Angelina.''

''A beautiful name.''

''Thank you.'' She smiled again.

His chest tightened and he found himself taking the folder. ''Look, Ms. Covelli, I should tell you that I'm—''

''Mr. Rossi,'' a voice called from the door behind him. ''There's a call on your phone. Your office in New York.''

''Please tell them I'll call them back,'' John instructed, then turned back to see the fiery look in Angelina Covelli's eyes.

''As I was about to tell you, I'm John Rossi, Ms. Covelli.'' He held out his hand. ''It's nice to meet you. Mark Learner, my assistant, has been singing your praises the past few months.''

She looked down at his hand then finally shook it. ''I apologize, Mr. Rossi. I know I should have waited until tomorrow, but I was hoping to be the first to see you.''

He cocked an eyebrow. ''So you were trying to get the advantage?''

She raised her gaze and stared at him. ''Whatever it

takes. But ask around, Covelli and Sons is the best for the job.'' She pulled out a business card and handed it to him. ''You will be disappointed if you choose anyone else.'' She pivoted on her high-heeled shoes and, with an arrogant tilt of her chin, marched across the lobby.

Unable to tear his gaze away, John watched the raven-haired Angelina until she disappeared through the door.

''Damn,'' he breathed, angry with himself for not being better prepared for Ms. Covelli. He hadn't planned on their first meeting happening like this. And the last thing he expected was to turn into a randy teenager the second she batted those big blue eyes at him, making him forget the reason he'd come to Haven Springs, Indiana.

He walked into the small room behind the registration desk. At one time, it had been a large linen closet. Now it would serve as his office for the next thirty days. Time enough to get the Grand Haven project under way, and most importantly, to be back in New York in time to spend the holidays with the only family he had, his grandfather.

And maybe by that time, he'd find out all he needed to know about the Covellis.

Angelina made it back to Covelli and Sons' office and collapsed into her desk chair. With a groan, she dropped her head into her hands. She had messed up everything, and her brothers were going to kill her.

She thought back to the fiasco at the hotel, and to the man who she had thought was the security guard. John Rossi had no right to be dressed in jeans and boots. He was from New York. A CEO for goodness sakes! Where was the three-piece suit? And he'd flirted with her, too. Wasn't there some sort of law about that?

She groaned again. She had flirted back. But a woman would have to be comatose not to recognize the man's good looks. "Tall, dark and handsome" definitely fitted him. How could you not notice his thick black hair and those bottomless dark eyes? At about six feet, he had broad shoulders that had no problem filling out his denim shirt. More than likely he worked out in one of those fancy New York gyms.

An alarm went off in Angelina's brain, and she pulled herself out of her reverie. Reaching for some papers on the desk, she began to straighten the stack. Why was she thinking about things she had no business thinking about? She didn't daydream about men. There was no future for her in it, hadn't been for a long time.

The memories weren't as painful as they once had been when she thought about Justin Hinshaw, her one and only love. A mere four years seemed like a lifetime ago…and she still had her whole life ahead of her. Still, she would never risk her heart again. "So stop thinking about things you'll never have," she murmured. "And remember what needs to be done." First and foremost, she had to never forget that John Rossi ran the company that controlled the future of Covelli and Sons.

The phone rang and she jumped. She reached for the receiver and picked it up. "Covelli and Sons."

"Ms. Covelli, this is John Rossi."

A lump formed in her throat and she swallowed it back. "Mr. Rossi," she choked out. "What can I do for you?"

"I'm calling to confirm a meeting with you and your brothers tomorrow morning. Ten o'clock is my first scheduled appointment. Would that be a convenient time?''

Oh, God. Angelina placed her hand over her racing heart. They were going to get the first shot. ''Yes. Ten o'clock will be fine,'' she said. ''Thank you, Mr. Rossi.''

''Good, I'll look forward to seeing you tomorrow,'' he said in his deep voice. ''Can't wait to hear more of your ideas.''

''I've got plenty,'' Angelina added, but controlled her enthusiasm, managing not to blurt any of them out on the phone.

''I bet you do,'' he replied. ''Until tomorrow, goodbye, Ms. Covelli.''

''Goodbye.'' There was a click in her ear.

Angelina replaced the phone and realized her hands were shaking. He hadn't called off the meeting. She smiled. ''He wants to hear more of my ideas.''

''Who wants to hear what?''

Angelina looked up to see one of her brothers standing in the doorway.

The second Covelli son, Rick, named after his grandfather Enrico, was the bigger of her two brothers. With his hair a little long, and dressed in black jeans and T-shirt, he looked like the town's bad boy—even more so when he put on his leather jacket and climbed on his Harley-Davidson.

Smiling, she got up and walked across the room. ''John Rossi just called. He wants to see us tomorrow at ten.''

''That's great, Lina.'' He hugged her. ''But I thought we were going in the afternoon.''

The last thing Angelina wanted to do was explain

her impromptu visit today. She shrugged. "Maybe he's scheduling appointments with all the contractors."

He grinned. "I don't care what time we go, I just want the chance to get in to see him. Have you told Rafe?"

"Have you told me what?"

The oldest Covelli sibling, Rafaele, Jr., walked into Angelina's office. He had on new jeans and a maroon polo shirt with the company logo over the pocket. He was more clean-cut than his brother, with short hair and a freshly shaven face. They both had dark, nearly black eyes and looked a lot like their father. Angelina could see them growing more like him each day.

"John Rossi wants us to meet him at the hotel tomorrow morning," she said, barely holding in her excitement.

Rafe blinked. "Are you serious?"

"Would I joke about this?" Angelina asked.

"Damn." Rafe sat down on the edge of the desk. "So we finally did it." He grinned. "We're going to get the bid."

"Of course we are," Angelina assured him. "I've invested too much phone time with Rossi International for our bid to be passed over. I've talked you both to death, even sent them pictures of every renovation you've ever done. John Rossi wouldn't dare give this job to another company."

"Rossi could bring in his own people," Rick said with a frown. "We've only got a foot in the door."

Angelina wasn't going to let her brother bring her down. "Well then, tomorrow we go over there and convince him that Covelli and Sons can handle the job." Her gaze shot back and forth between her brothers. "Come on, you two are the best. And you deserve to have this project."

Rafe and Rick exchanged a serious glance, then Rick spoke. "Rossi could refuse us because of...what happened with Dad."

Angelina closed her eyes, remembering not only the pain of losing her father, Rafaele, in a construction accident, but the humiliation of the false accusations that the company had used substandard materials. "But Dad was cleared. Peter Hardin confessed to setting him up."

Rick raised a calming hand. "I know, Lina, but sometimes people are still going to believe the worst about us."

She thought back to her impromptu encounter an hour ago with John Rossi. She had to believe that he was going to give them a chance and at least consider their ideas for the Grand Haven. He simply had to award them the job. It was the only way Covelli and Sons could get firmly back on its feet.

Then Angelina would finally have her independence—and the freedom to find her *own* career. Since she'd given up on love, wasn't that all she had left?

Chapter Two

The next morning, John sat at his desk going through paperwork and trying to keep his mind off Angelina Covelli. He tossed two business cards, one for an electrician and another for a heating company, into the trashcan. He would use his own people. It was the only way to insure the job was done right. The Covellis weren't "his people," but something told him they could be trusted.

John grabbed a pad of paper and a pen, and went into the lobby. He had a few minutes before the Covellis arrived and he wanted to make a list of renovations, starting with things that needed immediate attention. He took a quick trip around the hotel lobby, and realized just how many things there were in need of repair.

How could anyone let this beautiful place get in this condition? But John already knew the answer to his question. The economy and bad management.

Somehow, though, he would turn the Grand Haven

Hotel into a showcase and even make a profit. It would take a few years, but he'd get a return on his investment. Hell, didn't he love a challenge?

He started toward the registration desk and thought about the hundreds of people who had walked through this lobby. He'd heard rumors of politicians, presidents, even movie stars who had come to Haven Springs for the magical mineral springs.

Behind the desk were rows of boxes that had once held the keys to the nearly one hundred rooms. His excitement escalated. The place needed work, but the basic quality was already here.

Suddenly the front door opened and two men walked in. He saw the family resemblance right away. They had to be the Covelli brothers.

"Mr. Rossi, good morning, I'm Rafe Covelli," one brother announced as he held out his hand.

John shook it. "Good morning to you," he said, then turned to the other brother.

He stepped forward. "And I'm Rick," he said and they shook hands, too.

"Nice to meet you," John said, but his attention was riveted on Angelina, who had also stepped inside, followed by two other men. His chest tightened as she came toward him.

"Good morning, Angelina," he said.

She nodded. "Mr. Rossi."

Today she was dressed more sensibly in a pair of trim black slacks, a white sweater and a deep red blazer. John found he was somewhat disappointed that her dark hair was pulled back in a long braid. Then her clear blue eyes met his, and his pulse began to pound. It wasn't until Rafe spoke that he realized that he was staring.

"Excuse me, what did you say?" he asked.

"I was just apologizing for being late," Rafe said.

"No. You were on time. I arrived early." He had to get back to business. "I was taking some notes trying to get a picture in my head." He glanced around. "As you already know, the hotel has been neglected for a long time. Think you can handle a job this large?"

Rafe smiled. "Positive. I've been waiting to get my hands on this place." He waved the rolled-up plans in his hand. "I've been working on this project for the past few months. Ever since we heard the Grand Haven had been sold."

John nodded. He was impressed. Then his gaze fell on Angelina again and he couldn't seem to focus. He shook his head. She was definitely a distraction. He forced himself to look away. "I guess we…uh, should get started."

Rafe stepped up. "First I'd like to introduce our cousin, Tony Covelli. He's our partner and financial advisor. And this is Charlie, our foreman. He has worked several years for us and is one of the best carpenters around. But I want to assure you that Rick and I will be on the job and do the majority of the renovation. We believe that if it has the Covelli name on it, then Covellis do the work."

"That's nice to know," John said and turned his attention to Angelina. She was like the Tuscany sunrise coming over the hills. Hard to ignore. "What's your job with the company?" he asked.

"I've run the office the past two years. On this job, if we get it, I'll be the project manager." Her eyes flashed a challenge. "Do you have a problem working with women?"

So she planned on being around. "Not at all," he

assured her and smiled to himself as he thought about his indispensable secretary, Donna, and other high-level employees at his workplace. "There are several woman executives at Rossi International. I look at it this way. As long as the job is done and done well, it doesn't matter if it's handled by a man or a woman."

"That's nice to know," she said.

Angelina wanted desperately to believe him. She needed John Rossi to recognize her abilities. That had been the reason she fought with her brothers so hard to be named project manager on this job. And just maybe by the time the Grand Haven was ready to reopen, she would have impressed John Rossi enough with her qualifications that he would consider her as management material for the hotel.

"Well, how about we tour the hotel and you can tell me your ideas?" John suggested.

Angelina smiled as his deep voice sent warm shivers along her skin. "We're ready," she said. "Just lead the way, Mr. Rossi."

"Please, can't we be a little less formal and go by first names?"

She nodded, feeling nervous with his coffee-colored eyes fixed on her.

John then glanced at Rafe and Rick. "I want the lobby restored to exactly as it was in its glory days. It's perfect without any modernization."

Rafe nodded. "We only need to make room for the computers behind the registration desk. Rick and I worked out a way to hide them." They walked to the counter and unrolled Rafe's plans.

Angelina kept her distance and watched the exchange, remembering that yesterday this man was just a stranger in town who had flirted with her. Now he held the future of Covelli and Sons—and *her* future in his hands.

"Don't you think that you should be up there with them?" Tony asked as he came up behind her. "I mean, Rossi seems to have precise ideas on what he wants."

Angelina wouldn't do anything to jeopardize winning this bid. "Of course." She hurried to the desk and listened, then began to write down instructions.

Ten minutes later they walked up the stairs to check out the second floor where there were two ballrooms. The largest one had sustained weather damage, and the window frames needed to be replaced, the floors required refinishing and the woodwork would have to be torn out and redone. Angelina took down the details as the men discussed them.

For the next two hours, Angelina followed the men into several of the rooms. She listened intently as John told his ideas on the modifications. He wanted to convert some of the larger rooms to business suites, complete with fax and computer facilities to attract the area businessmen. But he was adamant that the top floor remain as large suites for guests who would be willing to spend the money for the luxury that the Grand Haven Hotel had once offered—and would again.

Finally they returned to the lobby. Angelina was about to head back to the office when Rick invited everyone to lunch at the family restaurant.

John checked his watch, then looked at Angelina. "I guess we've been at this a while. Thanks, I could use a break. Angelina, will you be joining us? I'd love to hear more of the ideas you started telling me about yesterday."

Angelina felt heat rush through her. "Sure. I'll bring

my notes.'' She managed a smile, but refused to acknowledge Rafe's curious look. No way did she want to explain to her overprotective brother what she was doing in a hotel alone with a man.

John read the sign, Maria's Ristorante, Authentic Italian Food. The converted downtown storefront was homey with its hardwood-and-brick floor. The murals on the walls added atmosphere and color and each table was adorned with white tablecloths and candles.

Lunch turned out to be a family affair—they all took seats at the large table near the bar reserved for Covellis only. Maria Covelli, a petite woman with warm brown eyes, came out from the kitchen and greeted her children and their guest. Rick's wife, Jill, a young attractive blonde who worked as a waitress, also joined them until the other customers demanded her attention.

Soon the table was filled with baskets of fresh-baked bread and generous helpings of Maria's lasagna along with a bottle of chianti. While they ate, John, Rick and Rafe discussed the finer details of the project, but John's thoughts weren't totally on business, not while Angelina was seated across from him.

At first Angelina let her brothers do the talking, but it wasn't long before John asked for her input. She felt shy, but knew this was her chance to show her stuff. She pushed ahead with her ideas. ''I like your plan for focusing on the business trade, but don't forget that the hotel made a name by catering to the rich. And if you're going to make the top floor all luxury suites you need more to offer, something else to draw them. Since people love to be pampered, I believe the underground area would work well remodeled with a new pool, spa facilities and a gym.''

The silence was deafening as she raised her gaze to meet his, and soon the dark depths began to mesmerize her. She glanced away. "It's just a suggestion."

John Rossi finally spoke. "Do you think you could write up a proposal for me?"

She swallowed back her excitement and nodded.

He smiled then, too. "I guess your coming by the hotel early was a good idea."

Angelina froze at the mention of her earlier visit.

"When was this?" Rafe asked.

"Your sister stopped by yesterday afternoon. I think she must have gotten her days confused, that's all."

John watched Rafe tense. Strange, they were all equal partners in the family business, but the men seemed also fiercely protective of their sister. Was a real family like this? Was this what he wanted to find out when he decided to come here? That the Covellis were a warm loving family?

How would John recognize a loving family? After his parents had died in an auto accident when he was ten years old, he had gone to live with his paternal grandparents. His grandfather had been obsessive about building the family business. His grandmother, a cold woman who busied herself with society functions, had ignored the little boy under her care.

John had looked forward to summers with his mother's parents at their vineyard in Italy. However, even though both Nonno Giovanni and Nonna Lia had showered him with attention and love, he'd never once seen them exchange a kind word, or a loving touch. John's ideas about love between a man and a woman had been formed at an early age, and he had never believed a permanent loving relationship was possible.

He looked across the table at Angelina. His gaze

locked on her shimmering blue eyes, then lowered to her luscious mouth. A mouth that made him ache. His body took notice, too, reminding him that he'd been without the company of a woman for a long time. He glanced away, suddenly needing to go outside for some fresh air to clear his head.

Just then, an older woman came walking toward them. Small in stature, she was wearing a black dress and her snowy-white hair was pulled back from her face. It dawned on him who she was—the grandmother, Vittoria Covelli.

When she reached the table, John immediately stood. The Covelli men did the same.

"Nonna," Rafe said and kissed both her cheeks. "We were wondering where you were."

She smiled. "I was in the kitchen as always, preparing the food." Then she turned her attention to John. "And who is this nice young man?"

John held out his hand and grasped hers. "I'm John Rossi, *signora.* I'm in Haven Springs on business."

She eyed him closely. "Nice to meet you, Giovanni," she said, using the Italian version of his name. "What part of Italy are your people from?"

John swallowed. "My father's family was from Rome," he answered. "Then, years ago they came to America, to New York."

Vittoria smiled brightly. "I came to America over fifty years ago...for love. I hope you are able to get back to Italy often." She looked sad. "Sometimes I miss the old places and the old ways."

Angelina spoke up. "You should let us send you to Tuscany for a visit."

Vittoria waved a hand. "Everyone I know is probably dead and gone. No one remembers me."

"You might be surprised," John found himself saying. "More than likely there's a cousin or two still around."

"Maybe there is." She cocked her head to the side. "You seem so familiar...something about your eyes..."

John masked his discomfort. He turned on his best smile. "Could be I'm one of your long-lost cousins."

Vittoria laughed and patted his hand. "You are a charming young man, Signore Rossi. We will be your *famiglia* while you are here."

John felt a tightening in his chest as he nodded. "You have fed me like family," he said. "And I want to thank you all for the lovely lunch. *Grazie.*"

"You're welcome," Rick said, shaking his hand.

"And I should get back to the hotel. I have work to finish," John said, as everyone seemed to crowd around him.

"Where are you staying?" Rafe asked. "So many places are closed around here during the off-season."

"Just outside of town at the Lone Pine Motor Lodge."

Rafe frowned. "It's more like the Lonely Pine Motor Lodge. There probably isn't another soul around. Besides, it's nearly twenty minutes away." The eldest Covelli sibling smiled. "Hey, why not stay in town? We have a vacant apartment just down the street. Since I was married last month it's been empty. It doesn't have room service, but there's a kitchenette and a big comfortable bed."

"And it's close to everything," Jill said, stopping by the table. "Only a few blocks from the hotel."

Angelina couldn't help but notice John's discomfort. Maybe he wasn't going to give Covelli and Sons the hotel job, and he didn't want to be indebted to them. No negative thoughts, she told herself. There wasn't another company around more qualified or talented enough to handle the project. They needed this job. *She* needed this job.

Angelina spoke up. "There are also two phone lines so you can hook up your computer and fax, and still have one free for incoming calls."

John looked thoughtful. "I can only take it if you'll allow me a six-month lease."

"You're staying that long?" Rafe asked.

"No, just a month. I plan to be back in New York for the holidays. But my assistant, Mark, will replace me and he'll fly down intermittently to check on the hotel's progress. So unless you need a longer lease..."

Rafe grinned. "Six months is fine, but you're welcome to stay for as long as you need. And it's ready now so you can move in anytime. I can have the key for you in an hour."

Vittoria spoke up. "And to welcome you here, I will make you something special to eat."

John Rossi blinked at the older woman's kindness. "*Grazie, signora.*"

One by one, the members of the family began to drift away, but Angelina hung back. "After a while you'll get used to it," she said. "They're all a little pushy, but they'll grow on you."

"You don't need to go to all this trouble," he said, his dark eyes sharp and assessing. "Covelli and Sons' work will stand on its own."

Angelina took a deep breath, trying to control her sudden anger. How dare this man accuse her family of trying to buy the bid? That hurt, and she wasn't going to let him go without knowing the truth.

"I guess they do things differently in New York, but our hospitality is just that. We have no ulterior motive. We believe our work will speak for itself, Mr. Rossi. We're just being neighborly, nothing more."

Angelina turned and marched off, praying she hadn't blown Covelli and Sons' chance of getting the hotel job. But, after seeing the surprised look on John Rossi's face, she decided it was worth the risk.

Later that day, John returned to his motel on the edge of town. Inside his room, he tossed his briefcase on the chair and went to the desk. He grabbed the file marked Covelli and opened it.

He'd done his homework, but he'd still been blindsided when Angelina turned up early at the hotel. He hadn't expected her, and he had desperately wanted to be prepared. One raven-haired woman with intriguing eyes and a sensual mouth had already distracted him, making him forget the reasons he'd come here.

John drew a deep breath, as a picture of Angelina Covelli appeared in his mind. As his grandfather would say, "such a *bella signorina.*"

He shook his head and brought his wayward thoughts back on track, turning his attention to the file. He knew that Angelina ran the office at Covelli and Sons. And according to Mark, she'd been enthusiastically pursuing the renovation job since Rossi International had purchased the property early last year.

John sat down in the chair. He had to say he was impressed after meeting the Covelli brothers. And they were experts in the field of restoration. The only other person who might have been better at this craft had been their father, Rafaele Covelli. And he'd been killed in a construction accident over two years ago.

John tossed the manila folder on the desk. How many times had he read over the same file the last four months? So many he had memorized it. But he wanted to know everything about the Covellis. More than he needed to know to hire them for the job.

It was how John Rossi did business. He'd learned it was the safest way to make sure people didn't take advantage of him. Not only in business—but more importantly, in his personal life.

He glanced back at the file. And this wasn't just business to him, it was personal.

The phone rang. He leaned forward and picked it up. "Rossi here."

"*Buona sera,* Giovanni."

"*Buona sera,* Nonno," he answered. His spirits brightened hearing his grandfather's voice. "How are you feeling?"

He heard a groan over the line. "I'm an old man. How should I feel?"

John grinned. This was the grandfather he knew and loved. But he *was* getting old, too old to run the vineyard alone. "Then let me get you some more help and you can retire. Come live with me in New York."

"I've grown grapes all my life. A man needs a purpose."

"But a man needs some relaxation, too."

His grandfather sighed. "You should take some of your own advice. You're always working—and always alone."

John and his grandfather were close. Though he was raised by his father's parents in America, John had always felt a special bond with his mother's family in Italy. Nonno Giovanni had been the one who taught John to cultivate the soil, to nurture grapes for the best harvest. And though John had taken over his American grandfather's business empire, Rossi International, memories of his summers at the vineyard would always bring him happiness. No matter what the distance, John and Giovanni had fostered their special relationship.

But when John had gone to Italy this past harvest, his grandfather had looked more tired than usual.

"How do you know I'm alone? Have you been sweet-talking information from my secretary again?" Donna Charles had worked for Rossi International for over twenty years. She was invaluable and knew all the ins and outs of the corporate world. But she also talked too much to his grandfather.

"A *bella* woman, *Signora* Donna. She only tells me what I need to know. One is that you aren't taking care of yourself."

"I could say the same about you," John argued. "That's the reason I'm glad you're coming for the holidays."

"*Sì,* and we can argue about this again."

"You are stubborn, *figlio.*"

"Something I inherited from you, no doubt," John mumbled. "I'm looking forward to your visit. In fact, I'm planning on being finished here so we can have a long uninterrupted vacation together."

"I would like that." There was a long sigh. "We both spend too much time alone. And before I die I would like to see New York again."

"You're not going to die for a long time." Even though his grandfather was seventy-six, as far as John knew the man was in good health. "I have to get back to work. I will call you next week. *Ciao,* Nonno."

John hung up the phone and wondered what he'd gotten himself into. For years he'd seen his grandfather's misery and always wished he could do something about it.

Were they so alike? In a lot of ways, *sì*. They both had trouble with women and relationships. His Nonna Lia had left Giovanni a few years ago, saying he had neglected her for years. That her husband had always belonged to another.

John had survived his own pain. It had been a few years, but the memory burned in his gut like an out-of-control fire every time he remembered Selina's betrayal. When he'd met her he had fallen hard and he'd thought everything he'd always longed for was within his grasp. He'd have the family he'd wanted since his parents' death. Then he discovered that Selina only wanted the prestige of being married to Rossi International's CEO.

Since then John had given up on love; it seemed a steel-coated heart was a family trait. He would concentrate on business instead.

However, for his grandfather, and to be honest, for himself, John wanted to find answers to questions which had been hanging over his family like a dark cloud for as long as he could remember. What he was looking for could be right here in Haven Springs.

The next morning, John carried his suitcase and laptop up the stairs to the second-story apartment. He used the key Rafe had given him to unlock the door. Once inside he was pleasantly surprised at the spaciousness of the place. The gray-blue-carpeted living room had a new sofa and two chairs. The kitchenette had a large table where he would have room for his work and still be able to eat. He examined the new cupboards, impressed by the fine detailing that was the Covellis' signature. Everything they did seemed to show a little extra care.

He went into the bedroom and found a queen-size bed covered with a navy comforter. The bathroom was large and had been completely redone with all new fixtures, including a double shower.

"Not bad." John opened his computer case, then found an outlet and plugged in the cord. In no time, he had hooked into the phone line and sat down to bring up his e-mail.

A crash from the outside hall drew his attention. "What the hell?" he said, hurrying across the room and opening the door to find Angelina Covelli on her hands and knees, surrounded by grocery bags.

She gasped. "What are you doing here?"

He leaned against the doorjamb, loving the wide-eyed expression on her face. "I believe I rented this apartment."

She sat back on her heels. "I meant I didn't expect you to be moved in yet. My grandmother asked me to bring over clean linens." She pointed to the grocery bag. "And a few staples."

He eyed her fitted jeans and blue sweatshirt—with Angelina nearby what other "staples" could a man need? Angelina was a sweet diversion from business. But he couldn't forget she *was* his business. He knelt down and began to help her gather food back into the sacks.

"You didn't have to bring me anything. I'm capable of taking care of myself."

"Try telling that to Nonna," Angelina said. "She insisted that I was to come here early and make sure the apartment got aired out and bring fresh sheets and towels."

John picked up the bouquet of dried flowers and caught a whiff of their sweet fragrance. He would forever connect this scent with Angelina Covelli. "Was it Nonna Vittoria's idea to bring me these?"

She glanced away. "They were from my grandmother's garden. I just thought a little color would cheer up the place."

"Thank you. No woman has ever given me flowers before."

She arched an eyebrow. "Just don't accuse me of trying to bribe you," she teased, then turned serious. "I want to apologize for what I said yesterday. I was upset because you thought we were trying to get the job by appealing to your stomach with some home cooking. Rafe and Rick don't need to do anything like that. I guarantee you won't find better carpenters to restore your hotel." She raised a hand. "And that's the end of my speech."

John smiled. So Angelina Covelli was not only beautiful, but fiercely loyal.

"I know." He reached out and took her hand and a shock of awareness shot through him. She looked just as surprised as he did. He helped her to her feet, then reached down and picked up the sacks. Allowing her through the door first, he caught a glimpse of her shapely rear-end encased in jeans. Funny, he'd never thought of denim as sexy before now.

John set the bags down on the table, then they began putting things away. Coffee, milk and orange juice. She pulled out a foil-wrapped package.

"Nonna Vittoria made you some orange sweet bread."

His mouth watered. "*Berlingaccio?*"

Her eyes widened. "You've had it before?"

"I *am* Italian aren't I?" he said, but decided not to elaborate on his taste for Tuscany sweet bread.

"Consider yourself special. Nonna doesn't make her *berlingaccio* for just anyone."

He found he couldn't take his eyes off her expressive face. "Be sure to tell Vittoria *grazie,*" he said, then asked, "Would you share some with me?"

She shook her head. "I really shouldn't..."

John went to the counter and stood next to Angelina. "Please stay. If only to let me apologize for my rudeness yesterday. I've found in my business you have to be careful."

She nodded. "Okay, but only if I make the coffee. And I can put on the fresh sheets while it perks."

"I'll help."

He finished unloading the bags and she put away a loaf of bread, bacon and eggs. He couldn't believe all the food. In New York his housekeeper prepared a few meals for the week that he could put in the microwave and heat whenever he got home. "I'm not much of a cook. Being single I usually eat out, or have something sent up to the office. So thanks for all this."

"Well, you're thanking the wrong person, because cooking isn't something I excel at. And it's got Nonna all worried. She thinks I'll never find a husband. Of course I've told her enough times, I'm not looking for marriage, I'd rather have a career."

"Can't you have both?"

He caught a sad look in her eyes before she glanced away.

"I'm just concentrating on my career for now," she said.

John shrugged. "Sounds good." How had they gotten on this topic?

His gaze moved over her shapely frame and his body came to life. He had trouble remembering what he was saying. He walked over to the table. "I haven't found any relationships that last," he said, wondering if she knew what she was doing to him.

"That's all I see. My grandparents, my parents, even my brothers, all crazy in love." She flashed that pained look again, then reached for the stack of towels and sheets, and took off for the bedroom.

He followed her. "So, if it runs in your family, why haven't you wanted to take the plunge?"

Angelina pulled off the comforter and began spreading the bottom sheet over the mattress pad. "Who said I haven't?"

Interested, he went to the other side of the bed and grabbed a corner of the fitted sheet. He watched as her delicate hands smoothed out the wrinkles. "Can't believe a guy would let you get away."

She tossed her long hair off her shoulders and looked at him. "It was a long time ago."

He stood by the bed, totally enticed by the petite woman across from him. He found himself wondering who this man was that put the sadness in her beautiful eyes. How could any man walk away from her? He ached to run his fingers through her silky hair, touch her flawless skin, to kiss... John shook his head. Damn, he was thinking about something he had no business thinking about. "Sorry, I had no right to pry."

Angelina couldn't figure out why John Rossi was so interested in her mundane life. She doubted he had spent many nights alone in New York. Women probably flocked to him. Haven Springs was going to be an awakening.

"I think we should keep focused on business," she said.

That was all Angelina felt she had left. Unlike her mother and grandmother she'd never gotten to marry the love of her life. Justin had died decades too soon. Now all that remained were memories that she could pull out on those dark, still nights when she ached from the loneliness.

"Then I hope you took me seriously about writing up a proposal on your idea for a pool and a fitness center at the hotel."

"I'll have it for you in a few days." She finished making the bed. "I've got to go," she said, then walked into the other room.

John hurried after her. "Aren't you going to stay for some coffee and sweet bread?"

Angelina forced herself to stop. Big mistake. John Rossi didn't, and he ran into her. She gasped as her hands connected with his solid chest. He gripped her arms to steady them both, but it didn't help. Her breathing suddenly grew labored when she looked up at his dark eyes. She couldn't move.

"Are you all right?" he asked.

She only nodded.

"I guess I should watch where I'm going."

His deep voice sent a shiver of awareness coursing through her, warming her body. The feeling excited and frightened her at the same time. She was definitely out of her league with this man. "I need to get home."

"You promised to stay for sweet bread, remember."

She felt the searing heat of his hands on her arms. His grip was strong, but gentle. She managed to free herself when she stepped back. "I don't think staying is such a good idea, Mr. Rossi."

He leaned toward her. "John..." he corrected.

"John..." Angelina's heart pounded in her chest, so loudly she thought he could hear it. She swallowed, wishing she could act sophisticatedly in this kind of situation, but the truth was she wasn't anything more than a small-town girl. She had to get out of this apartment, away from his alluring eyes. "Goodbye."

Turning, she swiftly headed toward the door, praying he wouldn't call her back, because for the first time in a long time, Angelina wasn't sure what she would do.

Chapter Three

Two days later, John stood in the hotel lobby with the security guard he'd hired that morning when the front door opened and Angelina Covelli came into the lobby.

He stopped and stared as she walked across the room. She was wearing a black print skirt that revealed the curve of her hips. A black jacket hung open over a red sweater that didn't hide the fullness of her breasts. Her silky hair was worn free and bounced against her shoulders with each step. She was lovely.

"Well, good morning, Angelina," the security guard said.

She smiled. "Hello, Harry. Are you working here?"

"Yes, he is," John said as he joined them. He hadn't seen Angelina in two days, not since she'd run out of his apartment.

"Hello, John," she said stiffly.

"Good morning, Angelina."

He couldn't believe he'd almost given in to the temptation to kiss her the other day. It would be a disaster for him to get involved with Angelina Covelli. Contrary to popular opinion, he wasn't that much of a jerk. Maybe he should just pack up and let Mark handle everything. But one look at this woman and he knew he wanted to stay. Damn it.

"I felt it best to have someone keep an eye on things since there will be so many people in and out of here the next few weeks."

"Probably a good idea."

Just then a messenger came to the front door. "Excuse me for a moment," John said and went to handle the interruption.

Angelina drew a deep breath and released it. She had the written bid in her briefcase, the ticket to her future—more importantly, the future of Covelli and Sons. She had wanted Rick and Rafe to come with her, but they suddenly had other things to do. Oh, well, she was a big girl, she could handle this.

Besides, seeing John Rossi at the hotel was safe, unlike seeing him at the apartment. She wasn't going back there. Ever. If something had happened between them, if he had kissed her, she could probably say goodbye to this job—and a future position for her at the renovated hotel.

Angelina looked across the room at John. He was dressed in black dress slacks and a forest-green sweater. She eyed his muscular chest and shoulders as broad as her brothers'. The man had to do more than just sit behind a desk to keep a body like that. Her gaze traveled to his square-cut jaw, cleft chin and deep-set sable eyes. His coal-black hair was perfectly trimmed around the ears with a slight wave across his forehead. He was so handsome....

Stop it! she commanded herself. She never ogled

men. Of course, John Rossi wasn't any ordinary man. Shaking her head, she tried to concentrate on the business at hand as John walked back to her.

"Is there a special reason for your visit this morning?" he asked coolly.

A little surprised at his curt manner, Angelina reached inside her briefcase and handed him a folder. "I brought by Covelli and Sons' written bid."

He took it. "That was a fast response."

"Rafe was working on this long before you came to town. I think you'll like the ideas he's come up with."

John opened the file and studied the first page.

Angelina stood next to him and caught the subtle fragrance of his musk cologne. She was reminded of the last time they were this close. She felt her heart accelerate and quickly gathered her strength and concentrated on business.

"As you can see, I created a chart to reflect the cost for materials and labor, floor by floor. So it will be easier to make any changes or additions you would like." She stepped back as he continued to read it.

"This is good. Very thorough, Angelina." He closed the file. "Have you had a chance to work up a report on your ideas?"

"Why, yes. I just wasn't sure if you were serious."

He looked stern. "When you get to know me better, you'll realize I never kid about business."

She wondered if John Rossi let anyone get close on a personal level—or was he all business. She opened her briefcase again and took out another file. "Neither do I." She handed him her four-page report. "I discussed some of my ideas with my brothers—only to see if they were structurally possible."

He gave her a hint of a smile. "You've been busy."

"I take my career very seriously."

He glanced over her file. "I'm impressed."

She should have been pleased, but she'd been hoping they could look over some of the proposals now. "The computer makes things easier. If you have any questions..."

The sound of footsteps coming down the staircase caused Angelina to pause. She looked up to find Gus Norton from Norton Construction Company. Oh no. She fought back a groan as he walked toward her and John.

The moment Gus saw her he grinned. "Well, well, if it isn't *Signorina* Angelina."

"Hello, Mr. Norton." Angelina forced herself to be civil and not announce that Gus Norton was a terrible builder, not to mention a jerk. He had continued to spread rumors about her father, even after his name had been cleared.

"Now, come on, little Lina, we've known each other long enough to be on a first-name basis."

She turned to John. "I better go, Mr. Rossi. Just let us know your decision."

"So your brothers are turning in a bid, too." Gus's eyes narrowed. "I'm sure glad you got that mess with your daddy all cleared up. 'Course, he did look mighty guilty for a long time."

Angelina glared at Gus. "Don't you dare say a word about my father...."

John cut her off. He stepped between her and the contractor, his eyes fixed, his voice steady, but Angelina could see his hands clenched into fists. "I want to thank you for stopping by, Mr. Norton, but I won't be needing your services after all."

Gus looked confused. "But I haven't given you my bid."

"I repeat, there will be no need," John said, remaining steady and cool.

Gus's gaze went from John to Angelina. "Oh, I get it." He grinned nastily. "Well, I guess I can't compete with what she's offering you."

It happened in a split second. John grabbed Gus by the shirt and pushed him up against the wall before Norton realized what had happened.

"Look, you piece of scum," John hissed in a low voice. "I wouldn't hire anyone who insults a lady in my presence. And if you think you're not getting the job because Angelina has something special, well she does—her ideas and her brothers' talent. They have some very good ideas on how to restore this hotel. So far, from you, I've heard nothing. I think it would be wise for you to leave." John released him. "Harry, show him the door."

"My pleasure, Mr. Rossi," the security guard said, taking Gus by the arm and escorting him out the door.

John turned to Angelina. "I'm sorry you had to witness that." Seeing her fighting tears, he said, "Ah, *cara.* Don't waste your time over someone like him."

Angelina shook her head. "I'm not. It's what he said about my father. He wasn't guilty," she insisted. "His name was cleared. But it still won't go away."

John reached out and caressed her face. "Shh, Angelina. It doesn't matter what that creep said. I know Rafaele Covelli was innocent of all charges," he whispered.

She looked up at him, her eyes watery. "You do?"

"Yes, I do," he murmured.

Then John lowered his head to hers, and Angelina

realized he was dangerously close. So close he could kiss her, and she wasn't going to stop him.

But Harry returned. "Mr. Rossi, Mr. Norton is gone, and I told him not to return or I'd call the police."

With his gaze never leaving Angelina, John said, "Thank you, Harry."

"Let's go somewhere to get some fresh air," John suggested. He noticed Angelina's panic and smiled. "You can stop worrying, Ms. Covelli. I just want to talk."

There was nothing wrong with just talking, Angelina decided. She nodded. "I know a place."

Angelina directed John four blocks to the city park. In silence, they walked through a grove of large maple trees whose leaves were all but gone from the branches. Although the sun was out, autumn was quickly turning into winter.

They continued their leisurely stroll until they reached the fountain. A cherubic angel looked heavenward from the top and water should have trickled down into a round pool below, but the fountain had been shut off for the winter.

Pulling up the collar on her wool jacket to ward off the chill, Angelina sat on the concrete edge. "My dad used to bring me here when I was a little girl. He said he named me Angelina because when I was born, I looked like an angel." She felt a blush rise to her cheeks. "Silly, isn't it? But it's something I keep in my heart." She sighed. "Dad's been gone two and a half years."

John nodded and put his hands into his jacket pockets. "I know. As policy, Rossi International checks out all companies submitting a bid on every project. I learned all about the trouble you had getting his name cleared after the construction accident.'' He sat down beside her. ''It must have been hard on your family.''

She looked at him. ''There was never a question about my dad's innocence. Not with us. We knew he'd never use substandard materials on a job. But to exonerate him we had to find the person who did. And thanks to a private investigator everything got solved.''

''Who did do it?''

''The son of a lumberyard owner. He was a drug addict and needed money to support his habit so he sold low-grade materials at top dollar, passing them off as premium goods. He's in jail now, serving a ten-year sentence for manslaughter. He'll probably get out on parole in a few years.''

For some reason, John wished he could ease her pain. Strange, he hadn't even known Rafaele Covelli. But he was getting to know his daughter...too well. ''Can you handle that?''

She shrugged. ''Nothing can bring Dad back. And Dad wouldn't want us to make our lives miserable.''

''That's a good attitude, but it may not always be easy to stick to,'' John said.

''Well, we've had years of practice with the curse.''

''Curse?''

She nodded. ''For over fifty years there's been a curse on our family. It started in the Second World War when Nonna was promised to one man, but was in love with another...my grandfather, Enrico Covelli.'' Angelina shrugged. ''The family of the man who was left at the altar put a curse on my grandparents. Ever since, Nonna has prayed that it would somehow end. Whenever something bad happens she feels she's to blame for it.''

John tensed. "Do you believe in this curse?"

Angelina stared down into the fountain as the wind lifted her hair. "On bad days, it's easy to use it as an excuse. But I don't think that my father died because of a curse. Or Justin..." Her voice trailed off, just as John wanted her to tell him who this Justin was.

Suddenly she was smiling again. "There's also been so many wonderful things that have happened to our family. Like Rick striking it rich in the Texas oil fields and returning home after so many years. Both Rick and Rafe finding love. The success of Mom's restaurant. The carpentry business coming back around."

He loved the way her eyes sparkled. How her mouth lifted at the corners. How she chewed on her bottom lip when she was nervous. "Sounds like the Covelli family is doing well. So you have everything you want?"

"Oh, there's always *more* to want."

He knew all about wanting, he thought as he reached into his pocket, pulled out a coin and handed it to her. "Then wish for it."

She looked at him, then down at the quarter. "Boy, wishes cost a lot these days."

"Inflation. Come on, make your wish."

"I'm not a child, John. I don't believe things happen that easily. Besides, there isn't any water in the fountain."

"Details." He waved a hand. "Maybe it is that easy, and we only make it hard. What's the harm in asking?"

She hesitated, then finally smiled. "Okay, I'll make a wish, but you have to make one, too."

At this moment he'd do about anything she asked. "Sure." He slid his hand into his pocket for another coin. "On the count of three. One, two, three." Both coins arched into the empty concrete pond with a clanging sound.

"What was your wish?"

"Oh, I can't tell you."

"Sure you can," he pressed.

"It won't come true," she argued.

"That's only when you blow out candles on a birthday cake," he prodded. "Okay, then I'll go first."

He gripped her shoulders and turned her toward him. "It's this."

John bent and pressed his mouth to hers. Heat pulsed through his veins as he finally tasted the lips that had haunted him the last three nights, making sleep a fading memory.

When she yielded as if she'd been wanting the same thing, his hand gently cupped the back of her neck. She made a whimpering sound and parted her lips so he could deepen the kiss. Another jolt raced through him. Nothing had ever felt so right...and so wrong. But he refused to think of the consequences. He had Angelina in his arms.

Slowly, he released her. They were both breathing hard, unable to ignore the reaction the kiss had sparked. "That's what I wished for," he said.

She shook her head. "You shouldn't have done that."

"Why? We both wanted it."

She stood. "That doesn't make it right. My family wants to do business with Rossi International."

"Then there isn't a problem, because I decided to award the Grand Haven renovation to Covelli and Sons."

Angelina's excitement was overshadowed by what had just happened between them. How could she have let John Rossi kiss her? She hadn't kissed any man since Justin. Suddenly her anger took over "If you think I let you kiss me because I was trying to get the contract...."

He raised an eyebrow. "I thought you wanted the contract."

"I do—we do. It's just that the kiss was inappropriate. It shouldn't have happened."

"As I recall you enjoyed it as much as I did."

Darn him. "But you caught me off guard." The excuse sounded lame, but it was all she could come up with.

"Whatever you say. I'm still awarding the contract to your brothers."

"But I don't want you to think...that what happened between us was meant to influence you."

"You mean that you were trying to seduce me to get the job?"

"No! You kissed me, remember."

"Exactly. It was just a kiss, Angelina. And believe me, I wouldn't be very good at my job if I let a pretty woman sway my business decisions. Of course, if you think your brothers should turn down the offer, I know that Gus Norton would be more than willing to take the job."

"You wouldn't," she gasped. "He'll do a cut-rate job."

John stood up. "That's just the reason I'm giving the job to your brothers. Because I know they're the best. Remember, I've spent several hours talking with them and I've seen their work. I always keep my professional and personal lives separate."

"I thought you didn't have time for a personal life,"

she challenged, knowing a man as good-looking as John Rossi had to have women after him.

He smiled. "Did anyone ever tell you you have a smart mouth?"

"No," she lied.

He turned serious. "Okay, here's the facts. I'm not giving this job away to just anyone. There's a lot of money involved and I trust that Rick and Rafe will restore the Grand Haven back to what it looked like at the turn of the century."

Angelina suddenly was excited. Covelli and Sons had gotten the job. Now she could move on, too. "I think it would be nice if you would tell them."

"Sure."

"Good, then come to the house for dinner tonight."

"Fine, I have no problem with that. I'll also look over your proposal."

Here came the touchy part. But she had to set ground rules. "I have another request."

"What?"

"You can't kiss me ever again."

That evening John walked up the steps to the Covelli home just as the sun was setting. The old Victorian structure had been immaculately restored in a quiet neighborhood on Sycamore Street not far from downtown.

He almost hadn't come. This whole thing with Angelina had gotten out of hand. All he wanted to do was restore a hotel, but he found himself lusting after a woman he never should have gotten anywhere near. Worse, she wasn't even his type. Angelina Covelli had marriage and family written all over her.

That kiss had been the biggest mistake. Now he

knew what she tasted like, how soft her lips were. He liked the fiery sensations she caused in him…a lot. Too much. He had to find a way to stay away from her during the next four weeks.

This was an expensive undertaking and he planned to make money once they finished the hotel. Right now he needed to get the renovation started before he was due back in New York to meet his grandfather. He needed to clear his head of all distractions—the main one being Angelina Covelli.

He had to stay on track, he thought as he pressed the bell.

Soon the big carved oak door opened and Maria Covelli appeared.

"*Buona sera,* John." She grasped his hand.

"*Buona sera, Signora* Covelli."

"Please, call me Maria." She escorted him inside. Maria was only in her fifties, a petite, attractive woman whose beauty was in her smile and big brown eyes.

He was ushered into the living room where the Covelli men had assembled.

"John, good to see you again," Rick said as he came across the room carrying a small blond boy who looked to be about two. John thought he looked about the same age as Luigi, his grandfather's vineyard foreman's child.

"Thanks for having me. Who's this little guy?"

Rick glanced at the boy in his arms. "This is my son, Lucas."

"Hi, Lucas," John said.

"Hi," Lucas said shyly, then buried his head in his dad's chest. Rafe came up beside them. "Lucas takes a little while to warm up to strangers. But by dinner you'll be like a member of the family."

Cousin Tony walked into the group. "There are several of us who have been adopted unofficially over the years. Hi, John, how are you doing?"

John shook Tony's outstretched hand. "Great, but I'm going to put on some serious pounds if I keeping eating your aunt's and grandmother's cooking. I need to start running again."

"Hey, I go out most every morning. Pass right by the apartment to the park and back. If I can nudge Lina out of bed, she goes, too. If you like we could meet."

An image of a blue-eyed woman tousled with sleep, her long black hair mussed, appeared in his head. John swallowed back a groan, feeling his body come alive. "Sure, how about tomorrow morning?"

"Fine. I'll leave here about six, be outside your apartment ten after."

"I'll be ready."

"If I'm a little late, it'll probably be because Lina decided to come."

"Come where?"

Both men turned to see Angelina enter the room. Her hair was pulled back from her face with gold clips and rested in soft curls against her shoulders. She was wearing a bright blue sweater and a pair of dark slacks.

Tony spoke. "John and I are going running in the morning. Want to come?"

She gave it a moment's thought. "What time?"

"Six."

"Forget it."

"What's the matter," John asked, "can't keep up with the guys?"

Angelina shot a glare at John Rossi. Why was he suddenly goading her? Well, two could play. She gave his perfectly pressed new jeans and green polo shirt the once-over. She wouldn't mind seeing him sweat a little. "Oh, I can keep up." She turned to Tony. "I'll be ready."

Looking surprised, her cousin nodded. "I'll meet you at the back door." He turned to John. "Angelina ran track in high school, even broke a few school records."

John looked impressed. "What were your events?"

"The eight- and sixteen-hundred meters."

His brown eyes held hers. "I was a sprinter in college. It'll be interesting to see how well we've stayed in shape."

Tony walked away, mumbling something about being left in the dust.

"We could jog over to the high school and run on the track there," Angelina suggested, wondering where her sanity had gone. She knew she'd been able to keep up with her brothers and cousin. But something told her she would never be able to keep up with John Rossi, and she wasn't thinking about a trip around a track.

"Sounds good," John said, "but I have to warn you, I haven't run in a while."

Angelina didn't believe a word of it. He was in great shape, and he was going to waste her. Bad. "I haven't, either."

Tony returned clutching three glasses of wine. "Let's drink to a little friendly competition," he said as he passed out the drinks, then raised his glass. "*Salute!*"

"*Salute!*" they answered together.

Angelina took a long drink. She had to be crazy for agreeing to this. She'd already gotten too close to the man—a man her family planned to do business with. For the next month, they would practically be working side by side. And she had to think about the future, a future she hoped would be with Rossi International.

John took a drink, then asked for everyone's attention. "If I may, I'd like to make another toast."

Rick and Rafe gathered with their wives as Maria and Vittoria came into the room. "First of all I'd like to thank you, Maria and Vittoria, for having me to dinner." He raised his glass. "Here's to the successful renovation of the Grand Haven. And it gives me pleasure to announce that Rossi International has decided to award the job to Covelli and Sons."

Angelina stood back and watched her brothers whoop and holler. They shook John's hand, then began tossing questions at him. She almost felt sorry for the man, but he was saved when Nonna Vittoria announced that dinner was ready and no business was to be discussed during the meal.

It was the usual Covelli get-together, plenty of food and loud conversation. Angelina noticed how lost John seemed in all the commotion. By the time dessert came, he looked ready to bolt from the room. Finally, Angelina stood and asked him if he'd like to step outside for a breath of fresh air. Rafe glared at her, but she didn't care. She escorted John from the table.

"I believe it's the guys' turn to do the dishes," Angelina tossed over her shoulder as they left the room and went out the front door. Once on the porch, they strolled silently toward the side porch.

She took one of the chairs and sighed. "My family is a little talkative. I'll just sit here and not say a word."

He rested a hip against the railing and stretched out

his feet in front of him. "That's quite a group in there."

"We take a little getting used to."

"I guess I'm not used to being in the middle of so much family. I was an only child."

Seeing his loneliness, she couldn't help but feel sympathy for him. "You must have been lonely."

He looked up at the moon. "I was when I was little. My parents died when I was ten."

Angelina gasped. "Oh, John, I'm so sorry."

He shrugged. "It was a long time ago. I came to New York to live with my father's parents. Grandfather Rossi began grooming me for the corporate life."

"Did you have any cousins to play with?"

He shook his head. "No, both my parents were only children. But I got to spend the summers with my other grandparents in Italy. There were a lot of kids around then, children of men and women who worked at the vineyard."

Angelina sighed, knowing too well what it was like to lose someone. "It's rough to lose your parents so young. I remember how difficult it was when I lost my dad, but at least I had my family there for me."

He looked at her. "You can't miss what you've never had."

There was such sadness in his voice. "Did you ever wish you had brothers or sisters?"

"Maybe a long time ago. But I learned we don't always get what we want."

Angelina's thoughts turned to Justin, remembering fondly what a perfect life they had planned together. She shook away the memories and turned her attention back to John.

"So I guess it's up to you to carry on the Rossi bloodline."

His surprised look made her realize how personal she'd been with her statement. "I mean, with no other siblings or cousins. I guess if you want a large family, then you'll have to do it all..." She groaned, feeling her face burning. "I mean..."

He grinned, then finally laughed. "I know what you mean, Angelina. But maybe you should stop before you dig yourself a deeper hole."

Smiling, she stood and walked to the railing. "Maybe it's safer if we change the subject." She found she was easily tongue-tied around this man. She needed to get on a safer subject. "I want to thank you for giving us the job. I don't want what happened between us today..."

"If you're talking about the kiss again, I told you it had nothing to do with my decision." More and more he wished Angelina had nothing to do with his ulterior motive for being in Haven Springs. What would she think of him when she discovered who he was?

She grew serious. "It's important that we keep this business."

"It's already forgotten," he lied as his gaze went to her mouth. A mouth he'd tasted once and quickly discovered that once wasn't enough. "We only shared a pleasant kiss." He stood in front of her.

"That's all," she agreed.

"Then don't act like I'm committing a crime whenever I get near you."

John turned and stepped off the porch. "Good night," he called.

Once Angelina discovered he was the grandson of Giovanni Valente, the man who had caused the curse to be laid on her family, *then* she'd have reason to see more than just his kisses as a threat.

Chapter Four

Angelina groaned as she did her stretching exercises. She hated getting up; the only thing worse was a morning without coffee, and she knew she couldn't have any until after her run. She pulled on a pair of black stretch pants and a baggy sweatshirt over a long-sleeved shirt. It was too cold to run, she argued, but she found herself coming down the steps and into the kitchen. After grabbing a bottle of water, she walked by a smiling Tony waiting for her just inside the back door.

"What are you so happy about this morning?"

"I was wondering if I should take a picture of this moment. You're actually on time."

She gave him a friendly punch in the stomach, then they hurried out the door into the dim morning light. They took off at a slow pace and headed down the street toward town. All the while, Angelina wondered why she was doing this. She could see her breath. Besides, she needed to show John Rossi her business skills, not her running ability. But somehow the man seemed to bring out her competitive side. She had always tried to keep up with her brothers in every way, and even lately, things hadn't changed. This wasn't just a friendly run. She wanted to show John she could keep up and do the job—any job.

They reached the alley, and found John Rossi bracing his leg against a step and doing stretching exercises. He wasn't immune to the cold morning; he had on a sweatshirt and sweatpants, too. With a nod, he joined them. Tony led the way through town to the park, then started across the street. As the high school appeared, so did Angelina's nervousness.

Tony suddenly stopped and grabbed his leg with a loud groan.

"What's the matter?" She ran back to him.

"It's my damn hamstring again." He winced as he tried to walk it off. "Sorry, John. Looks like I'm out of commission for a few days."

"No problem," John said. "Need some help to get back home?"

He shook his head. "I can handle it if I take it slow back to the house. No sense in spoiling your run."

"No, we should all go back together," Angelina argued. After what had happened at the fountain, she didn't want to be alone with John.

"What's the matter, Lina," her cousin said, "Afraid you can't handle some competition?"

Angelina wanted to wipe the grin off Tony's face. "Fine, hobble home if you want," she murmured as she walked by him. "Then after your leg heals, I'll make you pay for getting me up this early."

Tony patted John's back. "Be careful. She's fiercely competitive. Don't let her fool you with her compact size. Angelina holds school records.'' He turned and started his walk back to the house.

John looked at Angelina. She was wearing a Haven Springs Track Team sweatshirt. ''This is just an easy run, right?''

She smiled. ''Sure, but we don't have to run. This was all Tony's idea.''

''Since we're here.'' He kept walking toward the track. ''I could use the exercise.''

''So could I. Maybe just once or twice around.''

She began some stretching exercises and John was drawn to her nicely shaped legs. This girl worked out, he thought, appreciating the smooth, toned muscles of her calves and thighs. ''You ready?'' she asked.

John forced his attention to her face. ''Sure.''

They stepped onto the track and began to jog to the starting line. There were faint lines where lanes had once been marked. ''You should take the inside lane.''

She tossed him a smile. ''Since your legs are twice as long as mine, I'll take it.'' This was foolish, but John was competitive enough not to back down ''Twice around the track. That should even out the advantage a little.''

John figured he could handle that. Of course he hadn't been challenged on a run since college.

They both stopped and got into the starting position, then John called out, ''Go.''

Angelina took off, but John started out faster. She kept up around the first turn, then realized that he was baiting her. She needed to stay close, but not to burn out. Dropping back to her normal pace, she watched her rival, yet didn't lose any more ground. In her position right behind him, she had a great view of his smooth easy style, his long legs, his nicely toned rear end.

They finally made it once around the oval track and Angelina knew it was time to start making her move. Lengthening her stride, she picked up her pace and began to catch up with him. Not daring to look to her side, she concentrated on keeping focused on the race, but she could hear his breathing and feel his presence. John was a tall man, muscular but graceful, and he ran effortlessly beside her.

Two hundred meters to go; she could feel the pain in her legs and her lungs burned. She remembered what her coach had told her, *The wall is there, but work through it. Just focus on the finish line.* She did.

John watched as a graceful Angelina began to move past him, giving him a great view of her cute little bottom. They were coming out of the last turn, heading for the stretch and he was laboring badly. Hell, she was good, and obviously driven to win. Then Angelina suddenly stumbled and went down on the hard track. She let out a cry.

Panic surged through him as he stopped and went to her.

She grimaced with pain as he knelt down beside her. "You okay?"

"Yeah, just great." Tears filled her eyes.

He carefully checked the torn pants that revealed her skinned knees. His hands moved down to her leg and she jumped.

"Relax, Angelina," he said soothingly. "Did you hurt anything else?"

"No, I just got a little skinned up." She bit down on her lip.

John checked out her arms and found her sweatshirt

torn at the elbow. "Looks like you left a few layers of skin on the track. Maybe I should take you to the doctor."

"No, I'll never live it down if Tony finds out. Besides, I did worse damage when I fell out of my brothers' treehouse when I was ten," she said. "I'll just go home and clean my wounds." She tried to get up.

John stopped her. "I'm not going to let you walk all the way home. You cracked your knee hard enough to tear your clothes." He swiped his hand over his face. "Damn. This is all my fault."

"Why? We were both running all out," she said.

John could see the sweat on her upper lip. Strands of damp hair plastered against the sides of her face. She still looked beautiful. "The apartment is only a few blocks. At least you can get cleaned up before Tony sees you. Then I can drive you home." Ignoring her stubbornness, John helped her stand. He placed his arm around her shoulders and they started the slow walk toward town.

It took a while, but they managed to make it to the storefront alley before seven when the streets became crowded with people leaving for work.

John unlocked the back door and allowed Angelina inside. At the stairs she grimaced but started the climb. Before she could protest, John scooped her up in his arms and carried her the short flight. Her arms came around his neck and all she could do was hold on.

Upstairs he set her down and unlocked the door. "I never should have agreed to a race." He tried to hide a smile. "If I had known how good you were, I would have changed my mind. As you saw I had trouble keeping up."

"I also lied," she admitted. "I've been running the

past two weeks. It's a good thing too—your legs are miles longer than mine." She grinned, "But I was going to beat you."

"You're brutal on the male ego."

"Like your ego needs stroking, Mr. Successful Corporate Executive." Her blue eyes widened. "Oh, gosh. I'm sorry, John. I didn't mean to say that. I mean...since I work for you."

Smiling, he directed her to a chair at the kitchen table and made her sit down. "Don't worry about it." He went to the refrigerator, then pulled out some ice. "I like a person who speaks their mind. Besides, right now we aren't working. And the accident was still my fault." He came back to the table and gently placed the bag of ice on her knee. "This should help the swelling."

Angelina's hand covered his. "And I told you that you didn't cause my fall. To my grandmother's dismay, I've competed with my brothers since I was a child. She's been hoping I'd outgrown my tomboy tendencies by now."

"And she wants you to cook?"

She nodded.

"Did you run in college?"

There was the sad look again. "I did the first two years." Her eyes had a faraway look, as if she were remembering a difficult time in her life. "I kind of lost my desire. I decided to concentrate on my degree and a career."

"And you seem to be doing a good job. Your family business is thriving."

"Thanks to you giving us the hotel job. But it's time I moved on. Away from my brothers. I need my own space...my own life."

John knew that Angelina had been relentless about going after the hotel bid. She'd convinced Mark to read their company resume. His assistant had been impressed and had brought it to John. That's when he had first seen the Covelli name and wondered if they were the same family that had come from Tuscany, Italy.

John began his quest. It was an obsession—to find and meet the family who had caused his grandfather so much pain. Now, with one look at Angelina, he realized that he was getting too close. She had had him distracted since the first time they'd met.

He removed the ice, then lifted the stretch fabric away from her scratches to examine the bloody wounds that marred her legs.

"I hope you don't keep having these accidents every time we get together."

"I promise I won't do any running in the hotel."

John caught the twinkle in her mesmerizing eyes. Eyes that had haunted him since the second he'd met her. He ached to touch her soft skin, to taste that sweet mouth of hers again. All at once, his common sense returned and he stood. "Your brother has some bandages in the bathroom medicine cabinet. I'll be right back." He went into the bedroom.

Angelina let out a long breath and sank back into the chair. The burning in her legs was forgotten as she concentrated on slowing her pounding heart. What was she doing with this man? She wanted an opportunity for a job with Rossi International, and their relationship was definitely not headed in that direction.

Justin had been the only man she had ever seriously cared for. But the thought of John's gentle touch, the kiss they'd shared in the park clouded her reason. Soon feelings of betrayal engulfed her. No. This couldn't happen. Panic rushed through her and she realized she had to get away from John—from temptation. She stood and, ignoring the pain in her legs, hurried out the door.

John returned from the bathroom to find Angelina gone. Damn, what was she doing? He dumped the medical supplies on the table and had started after her when his phone rang.

"The hell with her stubbornness," he said. "Let her get home on her own."

He grabbed the phone. "Rossi here."

"Well, you're in a cheerful mood this morning."

John couldn't help but smile at the sound of his secretary's voice.

"You know, Donna, unless I see your face first thing every day, life's just not the same."

There was a snorting sound over the phone. "No wonder you haven't had a date in months," she said. "You really should work on your lines, John. Maybe take a few lessons from Nonno Giovanni."

"If you're wise you won't believe a word he says."

"I don't, only half of it." She sighed. "The man is so charming."

John knew that over the years, his grandfather and Donna had developed a long-term relationship over the phone. In a few weeks, he hoped, they would finally get to meet. "Did you just call to tell me my shortcomings, or can't the office survive without me?"

"I've got Mark handling things just fine."

He grinned. "I bet you do. So what else is going on I should know about?"

"Just that the stockholders' meeting has been pushed up to late tomorrow afternoon."

John frowned. "Damn. I thought we had till Friday to prepare. I just awarded the contract to Covelli and Sons. I wanted a few days to get things moving. Why the change?"

"Mrs. Rossi couldn't make it Friday. She wants to fly down to Palm Beach earlier than planned."

"Let me guess, she contacted all the other stockholders and demanded the meeting be pushed forward. So she wants a little power struggle," he murmured. His grandmother was the largest stockholder in the company since Grandfather Rossi had died five years ago and left John as CEO. They'd never gotten along, even when he'd been a small boy. Maybe she could never love another child after her only son had been killed in the automobile accident. Now, she had to let him know that she still controlled things.

"Should I send the plane?" Donna asked.

John sighed, but his mind wasn't on business. Had Angelina made it home yet? "Yes, have Gene waiting at the airport by eleven. Tell Mark to have the legal department draw up the renovation contract for Covelli and Sons, then overnight courier it to me. I want everything signed before I leave for New York tomorrow morning."

"That's cutting it close."

"I'll be there. Tell my grandmother to expect me." He hung up the phone. Stripping off his clothes, he headed for the shower. Well, he'd done it. He'd joined forces with the enemy.

Angelina was met at the back door by Nonna Vittoria, who took one look at her granddaughter and began chattering in Italian.

"Nonna, I'm fine," Angelina assured her. "I fell and skinned my knees. I just need to get cleaned up."

"Sit," Nonna ordered.

Angelina obeyed and took a chair at the large kitchen table. "Maybe I should shower first. Make sure that I clean off the dirt."

Nonna returned to the table with a soapy cloth. Her hands were gentle as she cleaned the wounds, then added an antiseptic along with bandages. When Angelina stood, she could still feel the soreness, but she had to get to work. It was already seven-thirty. She wanted to be at the office by eight.

"How did this happen?"

"I went running with Tony this morning."

"Antonio came back nearly an hour ago. He said he hurt his leg."

"Well, I decided to stay and run with John."

Her grandmother raised her knowing gaze to her. "Giovanni Rossi?"

Angelina nodded. "I came around the track and stepped on a rock or something. Next thing I knew I was going down."

Nonna shook her head. "When are you going to stop playing with boys? No, they are grown men. And you are a grown woman. How do you expect to find a husband when you act like a tomboy?"

Angelina stiffened. "I'm not looking for a *man.* I'm only thinking about a career."

Angelina let her grandmother ramble on in Italian until she heard the name *Rossi,* then she didn't want to listen any more. She walked to the doorway. "I have to get to work."

"You need to think about living. It's not right that you are alone."

Angelina turned around. It had taken her a long time to be able to think about Justin without crying her eyes out. Now she had fond memories. "I loved someone once, Nonna. But he's gone...." Her voice softened to a whisper. "I have my family and career."

Vittoria went to her granddaughter and hugged her. "I know, *figlia* child. But you're so young. Justin would not want you to deny love in your life."

Angelina was never going to love again. The risk was too great. "Just as Nonno Enrico was your only love, Nonna, Justin was mine." She turned and left the room, promising herself that she was going to concentrate on getting the hotel project off the ground. And showing John Rossi her business talents.

Then she could move on with her life. Alone.

Angelina walked into the office at ten after eight. The first thing she heard were voices coming from the conference room. She peeked her head inside and saw both her brothers and Tony talking with John Rossi. Her heart stopped. Why was there a meeting going on that she hadn't been told about? She was the project manager.

Rafe looked up and saw her. "Lina, you're here." He got up. "Come and join us. John called an emergency meeting and when I phoned the house, Nonna said you were in the shower." He smiled. "We were just waiting for you."

John could see that Angelina didn't look convinced. "It was my decision to call the meeting," John said. "I have to leave for New York tomorrow and needed to get the renovations going. But we couldn't start until I had the project manager here."

Angelina finally smiled. "I appreciate that." She set

her briefcase down and pulled off her coat, revealing a cherry-red sweater that caressed her breasts and was tucked neatly into a pair of dark pleated slacks. After this morning he knew what was hidden underneath.

"How are your wounds?"

Everyone turned to her. Her face reddened. "They're fine."

"What wounds?" Rafe asked.

"I took a spill when I was running this morning. I got a few scratches. That's all."

"Just so you got them cleaned," John said. "I wouldn't want you to get an infection."

She glared at him. "I said I was fine. Now can we get back to business?"

John smiled. "Fine with me." He turned to Rafe and Rick. "I'm having the contracts sent tomorrow. I prefer to have everything signed before the work begins. I'll be gone until Monday, but I want construction under way as soon as you sign on the dotted line." He glanced around the room. "Is there a problem with that?"

They all shook their heads.

Rafe spoke up. "Since the construction business is slow in the winter we shouldn't have any problem getting the extra men for the crew. They'll enjoy working inside for a change. We'll start on the second-floor ballroom."

John nodded and quickly glanced down at his notes. Damn. Every time he looked at Angelina, he lost his train of thought.

"We've agreed to the money amount on the bid. As for completion dates, I would like to open the first two floors by spring. The second-floor ballrooms along with the business suites could bring in revenue, and we can continue on the other two floors. We'll do them as phase I and phase II." He handed out copies of the plan.

After some discussion, they'd all agreed on the plan. Angelina was the one who had the questions. He had to admit he was surprised at her perception.

"So you'll be starting tomorrow?" John confirmed.

"Yes. With a full crew by the end of the week," Angelina replied.

They shook hands and Rafe, Rick and Tony left. Angelina went out to her desk and John followed her.

"I'll bring the contract by tomorrow."

She nodded, but her eyes wouldn't meet his. "So you're leaving in the morning."

John nodded and wondered if she would miss him. "In fact I'm cutting it close. The stockholders' meeting is scheduled for four o'clock. As CEO I have to attend. It should only take two days, but knowing my grandmother, she'll make it as difficult as possible for me." He raised his gaze to met her curious eyes.

Angelina swallowed. "Why would she do that?"

"I think it's because my grandfather put me in charge of the company. Maybe it's because I have her son's job."

"But your father died."

"And I lived," John said angrily, then regretted the slip. He never revealed anything personal about himself.

Their eyes locked, and he felt a tightening in his chest. "How are your knees feeling?"

She shrugged. "A little sore, but healing nicely."

"You could stay home a few days. I could call you there if we need to talk."

"For goodness sakes, they're only skinned knees. I'm needed here. Besides, I've got to hire a crew."

"Is my early starting date causing you too much trouble?"

Angelina smiled. Of course he was causing her trouble. It seemed her entire life had been turned upside down since he arrived in town. "No, there are plenty of men who will be grateful to get steady work."

With a wicked gleam in his dark eyes, he strolled to her desk, sat on the edge and looked at her. He was close, too close. She could feel his warmth, smell the familiar scent she recalled from this morning.

"I was thinking about *you,*" he said. His voice had a soft, husky quality.

Angelina found she couldn't move. "I'll be fine. I like staying busy."

"A *bella signorina* should have more than work. Don't you have any dreams? Husband? Children?"

"That's not what I want. Besides I have no time for those kinds of dreams."

He shook his head. "Such a shame, *cara.*" He took her hand in his. "You should take time for other things. Pleasurable things."

His touch was warm and gentle. A longing erupted inside her, one that she had thought was buried deep in the past, one that she had ignored for the last two years. Now John Rossi was making her aware of the fact that she was a woman. A woman with desires. A warning signal went off and she pulled back. "I don't have time for meaningless pleasures."

Chapter Five

John stared out his office window, down twenty-eight floors to Central Park. The trees were bare of any leaves, reminding him of last week and the afternoon he'd spent at the park with Angelina.

Turning away from the window, he sat down at his desk. He'd only been gone five days, but it had seemed longer. Even two days arguing with his grandmother hadn't distracted his thoughts from Angelina Covelli.

He found he'd been thinking about her way too much. How her smile lit up her face; how her blue eyes simmered with fire when she thought she was right. And she didn't give in easily. She was competitive, with an unexpected business savvy. She took an active part in everything that happened with Covelli and Sons.

By the time he'd arrived at the office that last morning, the Covellis' lawyer had already gone over the contract and agreed everything was in order. But still Angelina had questions.

He smiled, remembering the beautiful Ms. Covelli

seated at the head of the table in the conference room as if she were holding court. After thirty minutes, satisfied with every clause, she finally signed on the bottom line.

John hadn't been sure what he'd find when he arrived in Indiana that first day, but he sure wasn't prepared to have the family open their arms to him. He'd like to think it was because of what he could do for them, but his instincts told him differently.

The whole Covelli family had him off balance, from charming Nonna Vittoria to her beautiful granddaughter, Angelina. John had trouble handling that, especially since he'd never experienced much family before.

But he had to keep thinking about his grandfather and the years of misery the Covellis had caused him. John wasn't out for revenge, or he'd never have given them a lucrative contract. Why *was* he around? Curious about the kind of family he'd never had? Curious about Angelina?

Too bad he couldn't get to know her, the woman, better. Even if the Covelli name wasn't enough reason to make him keep his distance, John knew from past experience with failed relationships that it was best to complete his job and leave town. He'd already gotten too personally involved with the entire Covelli family. Besides, he doubted they would like the fact that he'd lied to them.

Yet he still found that he worried about Angelina's feelings. Would she end up hating him if she discovered the truth? He recalled the day he'd left for New York. When she'd said goodbye, her eyes spoke of a longing that made him want to pull her into his arms and kiss her. A kiss that would have her missing—

wanting—him while he was gone. He'd never got the chance.

Every night he'd found he'd missed her, even ached for her, but he couldn't act on it. Anything between them, even something temporary, would be doomed before it got started. Maybe *cursed* was a better word.

A knock on his door suddenly drew John's attention. "Come in," he called.

Donna entered carrying a file. The brunette in her mid-forties had come to Rossi International right out of business college. Now, twenty years later, the place probably couldn't run without her.

"Here are the minutes from the meeting. I highlighted the areas you wanted to go over."

"Thanks, Donna. Does Mark have his copy?"

She nodded. "And I took the liberty of sending a bouquet of flowers to Mrs. Rossi in Palm Beach."

John frowned. "What did I say on the card?"

"I just wrote a note of thanks for helping convince the stockholders the Indiana property was a good investment."

John shook his head. "Can you believe it? She was actually on my side."

Donna smiled as she handed over the file. "Be thankful she's smart enough to know that you're the reason the company is making money. Have you returned your grandfather's call?"

"No, I thought I'd wait until I got back to Indiana."

"You seem anxious to return. By the way, how is the Covelli family? I've spoken a few times with Angelina. She sounds young and attractive."

"How can you know she's attractive by her voice?"

"Let's just say it's woman's intuition."

John gathered his things, not wanting to answer any

more questions. "Okay, she's not fifty and she's not fat." He started for the door.

"Wait. What does she look like?"

John stopped and smiled. "I think I'll just let you use your imagination."

Monday morning, Angelina bundled up against the cold weather and drove to the hotel to find her brothers. Inside, Harry greeted her and told her the crew was on the second floor.

She started across the entry, then stopped and asked, "Have you heard from Mr. Rossi?"

Harry smiled. "He calls in every day."

Angelina knew that. She just hadn't been able to talk to him. "Have any idea when he's returning?"

"He tells me it's day to day." Harry sobered. "But if you need to speak with him, I could call."

Angelina shook her head. "No. It can wait." There wasn't any pressing reason to call John Rossi. Things had been going smoothly.

"You sure?" Harry asked. "I have his direct line."

"That's fine, Harry, it can wait. I'm going to see what my brothers have been up to." She breathed a sigh of relief as she headed for the stairs. The last thing she wanted was for Harry to think that she had a personal interest in their boss. She only wanted a chance at a future job with Rossi International.

Angelina reached the top of the stairs and walked along the balcony railing until she arrived at the entrance to the grand ballroom. She stepped through the double doors to find a disaster. Stacks of old woodworking had been torn out and tossed into the middle of the room. The screech of power saws assaulted her eardrums along with the rhythmic slap of hammers against wood. Last week they'd hired six extra men to rip out the baseboards while her brothers concentrated on replacing the row of large windows along the west wall. That was where she found Rafe. She picked up a yellow plastic hard hat off the table and went to him.

He smiled as she approached. "You decide you were getting too bored sitting in the cushy office and come down to help with the tear out?"

"Hey, I thought Tony and I were the brains of the operation. You and Rick provide the brawn."

He grinned as he returned his hammer to his tool belt. "Nobody told me that when I signed on the dotted line. You come down to play with the guys?"

"I thought you told me at twelve I couldn't play with the boys anymore."

"Well, make sure it stays that way."

Angelina shook her head. "How does Shelby live with you? We're on the threshold of a new century, and you're still in the stone age. Get this through your thick head, brother, girls are allowed to play with the guys. And we're good at it."

He cocked an eyebrow. "But you got hurt."

"I could have gotten hurt if I'd been running by myself."

"My point exactly. What were you doing with John Rossi?"

"So it's not that I was racing, it's that I was with a man." She smacked him playfully on the arm. "Stay out of my life, Rafe. I'm a big girl."

"Not to a man like John Rossi," he argued. "He's more experienced."

Angelina jammed her hands against her hips. "About everyone in the world is more experienced than I am."

A big grin split Rafe's face. "Can't say I'm unhappy to hear that."

"Oh, shut up." Her faced flamed, remembering that she and Justin had put a stop to their lovemaking because they wanted to wait until they were married. But their wedding day had never come.

"Now, is that any way for a lady to talk?"

Angelina turned around and saw Leo Tucker walking toward them.

"Tuck." She rushed into his arms and hugged the tall lanky Texan. Rick's friend gave her a squeeze, then released her. "When did you get here from Midland?" she asked.

"Just this morning." He eyed them both. "And it looks like none too soon. You two fightin' again?"

"Just giving my little sister some friendly advice," Rafe said.

Tuck's gentle gray eyes examined Angelina. "I'd say this pretty filly is more than capable of taking care of herself."

Angelina grinned and reached up to the six-foot-plus wildcatter's face and kissed him. "Oh, I've missed you, Tuck. How are things going on the oil rigs? Making any more money?"

Tuck had been Rick's business partner. They'd done very well wildcatting in west Texas before Rick came home. Soon after, Tuck had shown up in Haven Springs, too. Rick met his now-wife Jill and decided to stay. Tuck shared his time between Texas and Indiana.

"I'd say we're holding our own. I've turned things over to our foreman." Tuck grinned, revealing tiny lines around his eyes. That and his sandy hair streaked with gray made him look older than his thirty-five years. But it didn't take away from his rugged good looks.

Angelina remembered how openly Tuck had flirted with her when he showed up in town eight months ago. He'd been the first man to treat her like a woman, and, since then, they'd been good, easy friends. Like a member of the family. He'd even invested in Covelli Enterprises to help get things started with the downtown properties.

He glanced around the room. "I'd say we aren't doin' too bad here either." He looked at Rafe. "Could you use an extra pair of hands for the next few months?"

"Sure," Rafe said. "Why don't you get settled in, and come back this afternoon? I'll keep you busy for a while."

"Take me to the office," Angelina suggested. "I'll fill you in on what's been happening around here."

"Sure. I have a few ideas I want to discuss with you," Tuck said. "Nothing urgent. Just something Covelli Enterprises might be interested in for the future."

"I like the sound of that," Rafe said. "Right now, I'd better get back to work. Angelina will bring you up to date. She's the boss on this job."

"You got that right. Now get back to work." She grabbed Tuck's hand. "Come on, you good-looking Texan, I want to hear all about the millions you've made on those oil wells. Maybe I can convince you that I'm the perfect woman for you."

Tuck laughed as he slipped his arm around her shoulders. "Darlin', you don't have to convince a man of something he already knows."

* * *

John Rossi stood in the doorway, his hands curled into fists as he watched Angelina standing with the tall stranger, a man she seemed all too familiar with.

Together, the couple had started across the room when Angelina looked up and noticed him. She seemed shocked at first, then she smiled as they continued toward him.

Angelina was dressed in a pair of gray wool slacks with a wide belt that showed off her narrow waist. A fitted blue sweater accentuated her full breasts under her navy pea coat. "Hello, John."

"Hello, Angelina."

"I see you made it back all right."

He nodded as his gaze flashed to her blond companion in jeans and cowboy boots. "We finished up last night. I flew out the first thing this morning. My plane landed an hour ago." Who the hell was this guy? he wondered.

"John, this is Leo Tucker," Angelina said. "Tuck this is John Rossi. Our new boss."

John took the hand Tucker held out.

"Nice to meet ya, John," Tucker said.

"Tuck is one of our partners in Covelli Enterprises, the downtown redevelopment company."

John should have been relieved, but wasn't.

"I'm just a silent partner," Tuck said. "I'm a wildcatter by profession. Since my partner, Rick, has retired, I've been thinking about doing the same. And Angelina convinced me that there are a few good investment opportunities here in Haven Springs." He pulled her close to his side and John tensed.

John captured Angelina's blue-green gaze. "She has a way of doing that," he said, feeling he was being swept away. He blinked, then looked back at Mr.

Tucker. "There are a lot of opportunities here. Hope that means we can work together to bring the tourist trade to southern Indiana."

Tuck grinned. "Sounds like a plan."

Angelina's heart was racing in her chest. She couldn't take her eyes off John. He was impeccably dressed in a dark suit with a white shirt and printed tie. He looked as if he'd just come out of a high-powered business meeting. His coffee-colored eyes locked with hers, mesmerizing her, making it hard for her to breath. She didn't want to admit how much she'd missed him.

They stood there for what seemed like an eternity, until they were forced to move aside for workers carrying out some of the debris.

"I guess we should get out of the way," she said as the power saws started up again. "Do you need to talk to me about anything?"

John shook his head.

Angelina was a little disappointed. "Then I should get back to the office," she said.

"Nice to have met you, John. I know Rafe and Rick have been anxious to get hold of this place for years. Glad things worked out."

"Well, Covelli and Sons deserved the job."

John turned to Angelina. "How are your skinned knees?"

She tried not to blush. "They're fine. Almost healed, thank you. If the weather warms up, I was going to start running again."

He raised an eyebrow. "Need company?"

Not if she had a brain in her head, she thought. Outside of business, she didn't need to be anywhere close to this man. "We're expecting snow in the next few days." She slipped her arm through Tuck's. "We'd better be going. If you need anything I'll be at the office."

John nodded. "I'll talk with Rafe, then get back to you later."

Angelina nodded. "Okay, then I'll be seeing you." She held on to Tuck as they made their way out of the room, then down the steps. It wasn't until they were out on the street that she took a breath.

"Whew, I wasn't sure I was going to get out of there alive," Tuck said.

She gave him a puzzled look.

"If I've learned anything over the years, it's not to stand between a man and the woman he wants. And I'd say that John Rossi wants you."

Surprise shot through her. "You're crazy."

He smiled. "I may be, but that man didn't want me anywhere near you."

"John and I are just business partners," she insisted.

"John Rossi doesn't think the same way."

"Listen, Tuck, there's nothing personal between us. There can't be. You know that. I don't want a relationship with anyone else...." She looked away.

Tuck hugged her. "I know, darlin'. Life has dealt you a tough hand so far. But one day that's all going to change."

She shook her head in denial.

He brushed back her hair. "Yes, darlin'. You got too much love to give. Once you realize that, guys are goin' to be lining up outside your door wanting your affections."

She tensed her jaw. "All I want is a career. When this project is finished and John opens the hotel, I'm hoping he'll consider me for a management position."

Tuck studied her for a moment. "There's more to life."

She took a long breath as they stopped next to the truck at the curb. "Not for me. It's time I was on my own. I've been out of college for two years, now. After Dad's death we all needed to hang together because of the business. But, it's time now. Rafe and Rick have moved on with their lives, and they're still trying to run mine."

"It's only because they love you." Tuck let out a breath. "I don't have family, so I envy you—having people who care. And if you were my sister, I'd guard you like a hawk. You're a beautiful woman, Angelina."

She felt herself blush. "Thank you."

Tuck touched her cheek. "Stop chasing off any man who wants the chance to love you."

The next morning was cold and gray when John stepped outside at six in the morning. He hadn't slept much the night before, and had decided to get out and run off some of his frustration.

He did his stretching exercises and took off down the alley, then turned up Vine Street and headed north with no particular destination in mind. He wanted to clear his head of everything, and that meant pushing his body to the limit. But this morning, it wasn't working. Angelina had interrupted his sleep last night.

After being gone nearly a week, he'd returned to town anxious to see her, but when he'd gone to the hotel she was with another man. John picked up his pace as he came around the corner and headed down another street.

Damn it! Why had that bothered him? He was in

town for a job and to get a closer look at the family that had hurt his grandfather years ago. Then he was back to New York. The Covellis wouldn't even know who he really was. He couldn't get distracted by a woman who would hate him the second she discovered he had Valente blood running through his veins.

His speed increased as he crossed the deserted street, his lungs starting to burn. He ran to the parking lot, then ended up in the city park. Arriving on the dirt trail, he took off through the bare trees, when he noticed another runner about thirty yards ahead of him.

A woman. She wore stretch leggings over nicely shaped legs. A big sweatshirt with a hood pulled up. When he got closer he realized the woman was Angelina. With a groan, he nearly turned and went the other way, but he was never a man to run from a challenge. And somehow Angelina Covelli managed to push his restraint to the limit.

Angelina sensed someone was behind her and moved to her right to let him pass. After her last spill on the track, she wasn't about to overdo.

Out of the corner of her eye she caught the runner moving up on her, but he hadn't passed her. A slight discomfort engulfed her, remembering a college friend who had been attacked on a trail.

She picked up speed, trying not to let her fear take over as she ran, but he'd been following her for about a half mile and he hadn't passed her.

She tensed, trying to remember something she'd learned in her self-defense classes. She'd better think quickly because the runner was gaining on her. Angelina picked up speed, heading for the end of the trail when her predator came up behind her. Too close. Suddenly she felt his hand on her shoulder. In a swift motion, she elbowed the guy in the ribs and took off as he dropped to the ground with a groan.

Then she heard her name called. She stopped and turned around to see John Rossi sitting on the edge of the trail, clutching his midsection.

She ran back to him and knelt down beside him. "Oh, John, are you all right?"

He looked up at her, his face filled with pain. "I guess this is what I get for sneaking up on you."

Her hands trembled. What had she done? "Why didn't you call to me?"

"I did, but I guess you didn't hear."

"Are you hurt?"

"Where did you learn to punch like that?"

"I took a self-defense class. A woman's strength is to catch her attacker off guard."

He groaned. "I'd say you got an A plus in the course."

She managed to push his hand away from his ribs and raised his shirt. His flat stomach appeared, then she spotted the red welt on his rib cage. "Oh, John. I'm so sorry. I'll take you to the doctor. Please, let me help you."

He placed his hand over hers. "I'm all right, Angelina. My ribs hurt a little, but nothing is broken." His brown eyes met hers. "And you had every right to hit me. I shouldn't have grabbed you like that."

She was so embarrassed. "I just got frightened..."

"You don't need to apologize." He smiled through his obvious discomfort. "I'll just know better than to ever sneak up on you again."

She finally smiled and sat down.

John knew he was in big trouble. He was quickly becoming mesmerized by this woman. Her eyes...her mouth… And she continually surprised him. "I thought you weren't going to run."

"I needed to clear my head."

"If I'd known, we could have run together." His gaze searched hers, probing the seductive depths of her blue eyes.

"We're dangerous together. One of us seems to always get hurt."

"Maybe we've gotten all the accidents out of our system," he said. He took her hand and brought her fingers to his lips. She gasped as he placed a kiss against her palm.

She tried to pull away, but he held fast. "John, you shouldn't do that."

He leaned closer. "Why, *cara?*" His breath caressed her face.

There were so many reasons. But at the moment she couldn't think of any. This was a colossal mistake and she could get hurt.

"We work together." She rose to her feet, trying to ignore the deep ache in her stomach. There could only be one thing she could take from John Rossi. And it wasn't love.

Chapter Six

The following Monday, Angelina rushed into the restaurant and headed for the table where both her sisters-in-law sat eating breadsticks.

"Okay, I'm here. What's wrong?"

Jill looked up and smiled sweetly. "It wasn't an emergency, Lina. Shelby and I just wanted to run something by you."

Angelina plopped down in the chair beside the petite blonde. "Why didn't you say that over the phone? I practically broke every speed limit getting here."

Shelby placed her hand over Angelina's. "We're sorry, but lately every time we've tried to get together, you're busy working."

"You can stop by the office anytime."

The women exchanged glances. "We did," Shelby said. "Twice. You were out, or at the hotel. So we figured you needed a break. Besides, you ought to be eating lunch. Rafe says you've been skipping too many meals."

"Mom's got him spying on me." Great, her family had been talking about her.

"No, we're worried about you."

"I'm just trying to do my job. I *am* the project manager for the hotel."

"We know," Jill said. "And you're doing a great job. But we don't want it to be your entire existence. You should make time for some fun, too."

"Oh, no," Angelina groaned. "You two didn't fix me up with another blind date, did you? I told you the last time never again."

Jill raised a calming hand. "No, we didn't fix you up with a date. We learned our lesson. This time Shelby and I have been putting all our energies into planning a party."

Angelina knew that it wasn't anyone's birthday. "A party?"

Jill exchanged another glance with Shelby, then nodded.

Angelina loved her sisters-in-law, but sometimes they drove her crazy. What in the world could they possibly want to celebrate? She froze. Could Shelby be expecting? A twinge of envy took her by surprise. Angelina would love to have another niece or nephew to spoil.

"What are you and Rafe celebrating? Maybe an addition to the family?"

Angelina watched as the slender brunette's face turned a bright red. "Right now we're just thinking about having a party at Stewart Manor in honor of John Rossi."

Angelina's mouth gaped open. "Why?"

"Come on, Lina," Jill began. "There are several reasons. Mainly, his company has taken on a big project in our town. He should meet everyone, like the mayor and the historical society committee. After all, he is refurbishing the most prominent landmark in our community.''

Angelina didn't want any more social situations with John Rossi. It was bad enough working side by side with him every day, but to have to deal with a social affair and try to act as if she weren't affected by him... The man could make any woman tremble.

Of course for John Rossi, it was business as usual. Still, since that day a week ago in the park, he'd made no more attempts at trying to touch her, to kiss her. So why was she worried? The citizens of Haven Springs *should* meet him. ''It sounds all right,'' she conceded.

''Oh, good,'' Shelby breathed. ''I can't wait to show off the house.''

''So it's going to be at Stewart Manor?''

''Don't you think it's the perfect place?'' Jill asked.

Angelina nodded. Shelby and Rafe lived in one of the largest older homes in Haven Springs, home to the former mayor. They'd worked hard to bring the landmark back to its original grandeur. ''Perfect,'' she murmured.

''And I bet you can't wait to see how John Rossi looks in a tux,'' Jill said. ''He's such a handsome man anyway, but all dressed up...''

Angelina already knew how good-looking John was. ''Does Rick know you're ogling other men?''

Jill grinned. ''Makes him crazy.''

''Rafe, too,'' Shelby added. ''It's wonderful.''

There was that twinge of envy again. ''You two are just too sickeningly happy.''

Jill tossed her a knowing smile. ''I bet if you tried you could make John Rossi a little crazy. When I stopped by the hotel the other day to see Rick, I talked to Harry. He said that John had Gus Norton by the shirt collar after he'd said something about you. Sounds to me like John is a little protective."

Angelina remembered that day. The same day she and John had ended up at the fountain in the park. The same day he'd kissed her.

"Gus said something about Dad."

Jill turned serious. "Then I'm glad John was there to handle it for you. And speaking of being there when you need him." She nudged Angelina and pointed toward the door.

Angelina glanced up to find John coming toward them. He was dressed in pleated navy trousers and a burgundy dress shirt. Even coming from a construction site, he looked like he'd just stepped out of a men's fashion magazine.

He smiled as he reached their table. "What a lovely sight. Three beautiful ladies."

"Hello, John," Jill said, smiling. "We were just talking about you."

Angelina's heart raced as he raised an eyebrow and his brown-eyed gaze settled on her. "I hope it was all good."

"Very good," Jill said. "We're planning a party, and you're the guest of honor. Please say you can make it a week from Friday."

John looked around the table, taking in the expectant gazes. Except for Angelina's. He suspected she had nothing to do with the party plans. Though it hurt, that was probably for the best. After realizing how infatuated he was with her, he had worked hard to stay clear of her this past week. But, like an enchantress, she only had to look at him and he was under her spell again.

"I'd love to attend," he said, even though he had planned on finishing up his part of the project by then and leaving town for the weekend. He could postpone his trip.

"Oh, wonderful." Jill and Shelby stood. "Now, we're off to make out the invitations," said Shelby.

When Angelina started to go with them, John touched her arm. "Would you care to share a late lunch with me?"

She hesitated, watching as Jill and Shelby hurried out the door, then finally nodded as she sat back down. John joined her. The waitress came by the table and they both ordered.

Once the girl had left, Angelina looked up at John. "You know, if you can't attend the party, Jill and Shelby will understand. Everyone knows how busy you've been and you probably need to get back to New York."

He watched her fidget. "The company won't fold if I stay a few more days." He leaned back and smiled. "You seem to be the only one who wants to rush me out of town."

She blinked those gorgeous blue eyes at him. Did she have any idea of the effect she had on him? How every night he lay awake aching for her?

"I don't know what you're talking about," she said indignantly.

No matter that he had promised himself to stay away from her—or that he was staying on in Haven Springs mostly out of curiosity. It didn't seem to matter. He wanted Angelina Covelli, and he didn't like it—didn't like the lack of control she caused in him whenever she was anywhere near. She was a temptation he couldn't seem to resist.

"There's something happening between us, Angelina. You know it, and I know it."

Angelina looked panicky. "No, there isn't. There can't be." She stood to leave, but he grabbed her arm as he rose from his chair.

"Whoa, *cara*," he whispered as his fingertips touched her cheek, aching to pull her into his arms, to kiss her until she admitted that she wanted him as much as he wanted her. "I didn't realize it was such a repulsive idea to imagine us together."

She closed her eyes, but not before he saw the pain in her eyes. "Oh, John, I'm sorry. It's not you. I just can't..."

John's heart lurched at the sight of her hurt. For all his experience with women, and all his trying to keep his distance, why was this woman finding her way under all the barriers? He couldn't let that happen.

"Angelina. For whatever discomfort I've caused you, I apologize. It wasn't my intention to hurt you." He closed his eyes and felt a shiver rush through him. When he opened them, she was looking at him, her gaze suddenly cool and distant.

"It's only business between us. There can never be anything more." She forced a smile. "I bet you're eager to get back to New York."

John fought his frustration. He would love to show her his life in New York. But that was impossible. "That's right, I do miss it."

"And your friends."

Outside the usual business acquaintances, John didn't have many close friends. "If you're asking if there is a special woman, there isn't." Why did he feel that he had to clarify that to her?

Angelina raised her chin. "That's right, you don't believe in love."

He answered with a nod.

Emotions flashed in her shimmering blue eyes before she turned away, then picked up her purse and walked out the door.

John watched her go. "Oh, *cara,*" he murmured. "If only things could be different." And for the first time in his life he truly wished they could be.

Instead of returning to the office, Angelina took the afternoon off and drove home. She walked in the back door and found her grandmother in the kitchen, baking.

Vittoria glanced up as she wiped her hands on her apron. "Angelina, what are you doing home?"

Angelina shrugged. "I decided to take a few hours off. I can discuss the wallpaper samples with Mr. Wolfe later today."

Her grandmother embraced her. "Good. You've been working too hard, Lina. Come, what you need is food, then some rest."

Vittoria went to the stove and turned on the burner under a pot of soup. "I know you haven't been sleeping at night. I hear you moving around in your room late." The older woman's dark eyes searched her granddaughter's. "What is troubling you so?"

Angelina shrugged and sank down into a chair. "I guess I'm worried about work. I want to do a good job."

Vittoria went to her and stroked her forehead. "These lines aren't caused by work, but from the pain in your heart. Is it because of Giovanni Rossi?"

Angelina wanted to deny her problems had anything to do with John, but her grandmother would see through that. She nodded. "Oh, Nonna. I shouldn't feel like this.'' Angelina glanced away, knowing she could never hide anything from Vittoria. ''We work together.'' Angelina couldn't forget what his arms felt like around her. How his kiss sent her into a whirl of pleasure.

''How does he make you feel?''

''I'm not sure. Just off balance.''

Vittoria nodded.

''But there's no future for us.''

Vittoria murmured something about the curse as she sat in the chair next to her granddaughter. ''Oh, Angelina, love is never easy. *La maledizione!* The curse makes it more difficult. I have prayed that things will be different for my children.''

''No, Nonna, it's not your fault,'' Angelina insisted. ''You didn't create the curse. The Valente family did. Besides, Rick and Rafe managed to find love. So did I once....'' she hesitated, as tears welled in her eyes. ''Mine just didn't last a lifetime.''

Vittoria pulled her granddaughter into her arms. Angelina welcomed the closeness, realizing how lucky she'd been that her family had always been there for her.

''I do not question God's will,'' Nonna said. ''But you can't live in the past. You need to move on. If that is a career, then you should—what you say—'go for it.'''

Angelina raised her head. ''You want me to have a career?''

''Oh, my Lina, I want you to be happy.'' She smiled. ''Maybe you'll even find love again.''

Angelina bit her lip to keep from arguing the point. ''For now I want a career. I can't always work with my brothers. I want my own life.''

Vittoria squared her shoulders. "Good. A Covelli woman doesn't give up. She goes after what she wants."

Angelina knew that that was what her grandmother had done when she went off to America with Enrico Covelli. "I'm not sure if I'm as strong as you."

"No, you're more so. You were the first woman in this family to go to college. You can do anything."

"Sometimes I'm not sure I know what I want anymore."

Vittoria smiled as she pressed her hand to her chest. "Then you must listen to your heart."

The next day, John sat behind his desk in his makeshift office at the hotel. He'd been trying all morning to get some work done, but so far hadn't made any progress.

The thought of one pretty, dark-haired spitfire had been invading his thoughts for hours. He'd never let a woman distract him before. Now, after a single kiss and a few brief touches, he was acting like a hormone-driven teenager.

He had to forget her. Get back to work. That was what had filled his life for the past three years. He didn't dream of someone to share his life anymore. That wasn't for him, especially not a Covelli. He punched the keys on his laptop and began to concentrate on the next report. When the phone rang, he reached over and picked up the receiver.

"Rossi here," he said.

"*Buona sera,* John,"

Hearing his grandfather's voice, John leaned back in his chair, welcoming the break. "*Buona sera,* Nonno. How are you?"

"I'm sitting around too much."

John smiled. "Then why not come to New York early? I'll be free to leave Indiana by the end of next week."

"How are things going with your new hotel?"

"Right on schedule. Nonno, this hotel is incredible. I think with the right publicity we could get it off the ground. We've drawn up plans for a wonderful resort."

"I have no doubt that you will make it a success."

"Thank you for your confidence." Nonno Giovanni had always been his biggest supporter. He'd taught his grandson a lot more than how to cultivate grapes during all those childhood summers he'd spent in Tuscany.

"You've earned it." John heard the fatigue in his grandfather's voice.

"Are you okay? You're not sick, are you?"

"No, I'm fine. In fact, I'm looking forward to my visit and meeting your beautiful secretary, Signora Charles."

"So you think you've charmed Donna? I've warned her about you."

"And I'll convince her I am harmless," his grandfather said.

They both laughed. John knew Giovanni would never admit it, but even though they'd been separated for many years, his grandfather still missed his wife, Lia. And Nonna Lia loved her husband, but after years of a cold marriage, she had told Giovanni she was tired of taking second place to his first love, Vittoria, and had left him.

"Oh, *mio figlio*. I am an old man. I will leave the romancing to you. Tell me you've met a special woman."

John froze as his thoughts turned to Angelina.

"Sorry, Giovanni. Looks like I'm a confirmed bachelor."

There was a long silence, then Giovanni spoke, "I didn't set you a very good example on love. I was such a foolish old man. No wonder I'm all alone."

"You are not foolish, and I care about you, Nonno," he assured him. "Don't ever think you are alone." Giovanni Valente had been the best part of John's childhood.

"You are special to me also."

"And I can't wait to show you New York. We're going to have a great holiday together."

"You shouldn't be spending it with an old man. There have to be a few *bella signorinas* in your big city."

John laughed, glad that his grandfather was once again teasing. "There are plenty of *bella signorinas.*"

Something made John look up, only to find a beautiful woman standing in the doorway. Angelina. She was dressed in a pencil-straight black skirt that emphasized the luscious curve of her hips and shapely legs. He drew a deep breath as his gaze moved upward to the white blouse tucked into the waistband, showing off her tiny waist. She had on a cranberry blazer. He took in her face and flawless skin. He bet she wore little makeup. Her own natural coloring was enough. Her blue-green eyes sparkled at him, causing his heart to race.

John gripped the receiver tightly. "I've got to go, Nonno."

"Sure, I will let you get back to work."

"I promise I will call you soon. *Ciao.*" He hung up the phone, stood and came around the desk. "Now what can I do for you?"

"I'm sorry, I had no idea you were talking long-distance."

He smiled. "All my calls are long-distance. That was my grandfather."

"Oh, I'm sorry," she said. "I could have come back."

He shook his head. "No need. My grandfather and I talk several times a week. He knows I have business to attend to."

He found himself staring. Angelina was striking. "What can I help you with?"

"I just wanted to know when your interior designer was arriving."

"I'm not sure..." he murmured, wondering if there was any time that she didn't look beautiful. He'd seen her at six in the morning in sweats and at noon in business suits. Every time, she'd taken his breath away. He looked in her eyes and saw her confusion.

He regained his thoughts and stepped back. "I believe Valerie said she'd be here on Friday." He reached for his engagement book on the desk. "That's right. It says, 'Valerie Peters arriving by the end of the week.'" What the hell was wrong with him?

Angelina nodded and looked down at her notepad. "Well, I talked with Bently Wolfe from the historical society. He's willing to meet with Ms. Peters and help select authentic drapery fabrics and wallpaper. The society has photos of what the Grand Haven looked like nearly seventy years ago. Mr. Wolfe entrusted me with several." She reached into her briefcase and pulled out an envelope.

John moved next to her as she laid out hand-tinted old photographs of the hotel's once-beautiful interior, the wide staircase with the highly polished oak banister and carpeting in a rich scarlet hue.

"*Dio,* it was magnificent," he breathed in and caught a distracting whiff of the fresh scent of her hair. "And that's the way I want it to look again."

She glanced up at him. He saw her eyes widen and heard the catch in her breath as she realized his nearness. "Now you can see why my brothers have been so anxious to restore it. I truly believe we can make the Grand Haven even more elegant than it was before."

Though he knew he should, John couldn't seem to move away from her. "Do you realize that when you get excited your eyes nearly turn green rather than blue?"

She didn't move, either. "Nonna said the same thing about my grandfather."

John shook his head slowly. "His eyes couldn't have been as beautiful as yours." His gaze lowered to her full mouth. He raised a finger and gently stroked its smooth surface. Immediately he was hungry for a taste. "I haven't found anything about you that isn't beautiful."

"John..." Angelina closed her eyes. "This complicates things."

He knew she was right, but he couldn't seem to resist her. He had to. He had to focus on his job. And to forget about Angelina as a woman.

"Oh, *cara.* I can't seem to help myself when you're around." He drew a breath. God help him, he thought as he bent his head toward her. At the last second, he managed to move away from her lips and place a lingering kiss on her forehead.

He wanted this woman, but he couldn't do a damn thing about it. Except let her go.

The next day, Angelina walked into the conference room at the office to find Leo Tucker calculating figures at the table. "Hey, Tuck, how would you like to do me a big favor and take me to a party a week from Friday night?"

He glanced up with a surprised look. "You mean the one at Rafe and Shelby's?"

"That's the one." She went to the table and sat down on the edge, crossing her legs, giving him her best sexy pose. "Think we might turn a few heads if we show up together?"

He gave her his biggest grin—Texas big. "Sure, I'm not half-bad cleaned up," he said, then gave her an exaggerated once-over. "But why waste your time on an old used-up guy like me, when there's a mess of younger men out there just ready for you to give them the time of day?"

She glanced away, thinking about John and what almost had happened in the office yesterday. And she would have *let* him kiss her. She pushed the thought away and looked at Tuck. "I'm not interested in a relationship."

Tuck smiled. "Darlin', if I had a dime for every time I've heard that one..."

"Well, I mean it. I don't want or need a man in my life."

He sobered. "That can make things pretty dull. But I doubt you have to worry about that with Rossi around. The man has been hot after you like a hound dog on a coon."

Angelina almost laughed. "You have a unique way of expressing yourself."

"I'm only speaking the truth. The man wants you."

She tried to ignore the shiver that raced through her body. "There isn't exactly a large available female population in town. John Rossi is just passing the time."

"There are plenty of good-looking women in town."

She touched his weathered cheek. "And I bet you've attracted every one of them with that Texas charm of yours."

He actually blushed. "Do your brothers really let you run around loose?"

She giggled. It was fun just to tease. "Maybe you haven't noticed, but I'm all grown up."

"Darlin', I've noticed, but I'm not the man you have to worry about."

She crossed her arms over her chest. "I'm not worried about a man."

"Men aren't helpless. I believe your mama taught all you kids to take care of yourselves." He leaned forward and cupped her cheek. "Just don't pass up the special someone who believes the sun rises and sets in your eyes. A man who can't bear not having you in his life, and who'll treasure every day the two of you have together."

Tears appeared in Angelina's eyes. She'd had that once and it had all been taken away. She couldn't go through the pain again. "Oh, Tuck," she whispered. "Why don't *you* marry me?"

The Texan grinned and slowly shook his head. "Your heart already belongs to someone else." He stood and kissed the end of her nose, then glanced at the doorway.

Angelina turned to find John standing alongside a tall blonde.

"John," she gasped and slid off the table. "I'm sorry. I didn't hear you come in." She glanced at Tuck. He appeared to be enjoying her discomfort.

"You seemed to be busy," John said. "I've brought Valerie Peters over to meet you."

Angelina held out her hand. "Nice to meet you, Ms. Peters. John has raved about your work."

"Please, call me Valerie. John and I have worked on a lot of jobs together. I pretty much know what he wants."

Angelina just bet she did. "Valerie, I'd like you to meet Leo Tucker. Leo, this is Valerie. She's the interior designer for the hotel."

"My pleasure, ma'am."

Valerie smiled and her brown eyes flashed an interest in Tuck. "By the sound of your accent, Mr. Tucker, I'd say you aren't from around here. Maybe Texas?"

"West Texas to be exact, and please, call me Tuck."

Valerie nodded, then turned to John. "John, I'd like to get settled in my hotel room before the meeting with Mr. Wolfe."

John checked his watch then turned to Valerie. "Would you mind waiting a few minutes? I just want to call New York."

"No need," Tuck interrupted. "I can take the lady anywhere she wants to go."

Angelina felt like a fifth wheel as both men tried to win Valerie's attention. Tuck won and the couple started out the door. He stopped and looked back at Angelina. "What time next Friday night, darlin'?"

Even without looking, she could feel John's heated

gaze on her. "Oh, about six-thirty. We should get there early, in case we're needed to help. Thanks, Tuck."

"No, thank *you,*" Tuck said with a wink, then escorted Ms. Peters out the door.

John stared at Angelina. "Have you known Mr. Tucker a long time?"

"About eight months. He's a dear man."

"And several years older," he murmured.

"Age isn't important. It's what you have in common, how you feel about each other. Tuck and I have hit it off since he came to town. Besides, he's considering moving here. He's a partner in Covelli Enterprises."

He cocked an eyebrow. "As you've told me over and over it's usually a mistake to get involved with someone you work with."

She raised her chin, betting that he'd gone out with Ms. Peters. So what? She didn't care. "Who said anything about us being involved?"

Chapter Seven

After fifty years, Stewart Manor looked regal and beautiful once again. On the night of the party, the high wrought-iron fence was draped in tiny twinkling lights, illuminating the long circular drive to the three-story brick home. An attendant hired for the formal affair rushed out to park Tuck's car. Another came around to assist Angelina.

"Good evening, miss," the young man said.

"Thank you." She took his hand and stood, then smoothed out any wrinkles in her long, teal-blue dress.

Two days ago, she'd gone shopping in Louisville and splurged on the shimmering satin gown. The fitted bodice hugged her waist and draped softly along her body, emphasizing her curves. She glanced down at the exposed cleavage and wondered if she'd gone too far. But the salesclerk had insisted the dress was perfect for her.

Angelina wasn't so sure.

Tuck came up beside her, looking handsome in his

Western-cut tux. His sandy hair was combed off his forehead, but she doubted the usually wayward strands would stay there for long.

He grinned as he took her arm and tucked it in his. "Darlin', if you're planning on doin' some huntin', I'd say that dress is the right equipment for it. And no doubt you're gonna find your share of wild beasts tonight."

Angelina laughed. "I don't think you have to worry, Tuck. Men don't go crazy around me."

"That's because your brothers have always been able to ward off unwanted advances." He eyed her closely. "But I have a feeling, with the way you look in that dress, things could get interesting tonight."

Before Angelina could respond, he walked her up the steps to the cut-glass-paneled door.

A man in a dark suit opened the door. "Welcome to Stewart Manor." He gestured for them to come in.

Angelina stepped across the threshold and into the large entry. She glanced around the beautiful room, from the glossy hardwood floors to the tall ceiling where a teardrop chandelier sparkled like stars.

In awe of the changes, she couldn't help remembering what bad shape the abandoned house had been in when Shelby had bought it at auction. She and Rafe had put a lot of work into the place. Tonight was the grand unveiling for one of Haven Springs' historical landmarks.

"We came early to help, but it looks like everything is under control."

"Yes, ma'am. May I take your wrap?"

"Thanks." She removed the black lace shawl.

"I'll put it in the study," he said, then disappeared down the hall.

A soft whistle escaped Tuck's lips. "This is what I call high class. They're pulling out all the stops for this Rossi fella."

"It's hard to believe that Shelby has done so much so fast." Angelina eyed the new floral wallpaper, the oak wainscoting. "The last time I was here, they hadn't finished painting. They must have worked around the clock to get ready for tonight."

She wandered into the front parlor to find a beautiful antique secretary desk, a Victorian love seat redone in burgundy brocade and two chairs that carried the same color. An Oriental rug covered the floor and new drapes hung in the windows, barely exposing the sheer curtains beneath.

A waiter appeared. "Would you care for something to drink?"

"No, thank you. We'll wait until the party starts. Are Shelby and Rafe around?"

"I believe Mr. and Mrs. Covelli are coming down now," the waiter said.

Angelina returned to the entry and looked toward the top of the wide staircase to see the handsome couple. Rafe was dressed in a black tux and his wife in a lavender sheath. A glowing Shelby looped her arm through her husband's, and they smiled at each other as they came down the steps. An intimate smile, as if they were sharing a secret that was meant only for them, and letting everyone know how much in love they were.

A twinge of longing struck Angelina. She would never have what Shelby and Jill had. A man to share her life with. Someone to make her laugh, to hold her when she cried…to make love to her as if she were the only woman in the world.

"They make a handsome couple," a male voice murmured.

Angelina swung around to find John standing behind her. "Oh, I didn't see you come in."

"I'd say you were distracted," he said as his own gaze swept over her. "Such a *bella signorina.*"

She felt a warm rush go through her. *"Grazie"* she managed. "You look very nice yourself." The black tux was custom-made, no doubt, she thought. His snowy-white pleated dress shirt accentuated his olive skin and black wavy hair. He was handsome and relaxed in the formal attire, making her realize how different they really were. John Rossi probably had attended hundreds of these gatherings in New York. The party tonight would be the talk of Haven Springs for years. Their lives were different, indeed.

Angelina glanced away to break the hold his mesmerizing gaze had on her. Could it be that difference was what made him so intriguing? Whatever the reason, she had to stop looking at him as a man. He was a business associate and, she hoped, some day her employer.

She smiled and turned back to him. "Shelby and Jill have worked very hard to make this evening a success. I hope everything turns out."

He frowned. "I realize Rafe and Shelby went to a lot of trouble. But they didn't have to on my account. I would have enjoyed myself as much if they had barbecued hamburgers in the backyard."

Angelina doubted that, but she kept her mouth shut. Tuck came up to her, bringing along Rafe and Shelby. To Angelina's relief, the conversation shifted to hotel business. The rest of her family arrived, Rick and Jill and her mother. Her nonna had stayed at home to watch little Lucas.

Jill wore a shimmering black sheath that almost concealed her early pregnancy. Rick was handsome in his tux, his long hair giving him a roguish look.

But Maria Covelli was the one who drew the attention. Angelina's mother was wearing a rose-colored evening dress that emphasized her hourglass figure. Several men seemed to notice also.

"You look wonderful, Mom," Angelina said.

"I think we all look pretty nice, including my sons." Maria smiled and glanced around the entry as more and more guests came in. "It's fun getting all dressed up."

Angelina glanced at John. "Yes, it is," she answered.

The other guests seemed to be having a great time. When they came up to meet John, he quickly put them at ease with conversation about the town or questions about their families.

"Isn't John wonderful?" Jill said as she pulled Angelina away. "And so handsome. I mean Rick is handsome, but this guy is so cool. He never looks ruffled."

Angelina had noticed. "And he definitely knows how to work a crowd," she said.

"But he's so genuine."

Angelina watched as John paid close attention to each and every guest, especially the women. "He's in the hotel business. He has to be able to turn on the charm."

Jill studied Angelina. "If I didn't know better I'd say you were jealous."

Angelina gasped. "I'm not jealous." She lowered her eyes. "I'm not interested in him in any way but for—"

"—business," Jill finished. "If that's so, why did you spend a fortune on a sexy dress?"

A blushing Angelina opened her mouth, then closed it. She had no answer.

Her sister-in-law gazed down at the dress in question. "As your brother would say, 'you sure got your money's worth.' Several men have been staring at you. And there's more than one good catch out there, so stop frowning."

"I don't want to catch anything, especially a man."

Jill studied her for a moment. "Look, Lina. I know what Justin meant to you. How much you cared for him. But don't give up on living."

"But—"

No," Jill stopped Angelina's words. "I was where you are just about eight months ago. No way was I going to let your brother get close. I was afraid I'd be hurt or Lucas would be hurt again, and I almost lost my chance at love. Don't let fear hold back your feelings, Angelina. Especially when I see the way John's been looking in your direction about every thirty seconds. I'd say that he's more than noticed you."

Angelina's heart began to drum in her chest. She looked across the room as John shook hands with the mayor and some of the city councillors. Then suddenly his dark-eyed gaze caught hers, causing her both excitement and aggravation. She didn't want to want this man. Yet she couldn't seem to help herself. Taking a shaky breath, she started toward him.

Immediately John smiled and reached for her hand. A warmth shot through Angelina as he drew her to his side.

"This is the person I'm grateful to," he announced to the group. "Angelina has taken control of this project and gotten things moving on time. She's unbelievable. Haven Springs owes her its gratitude."

"You're exaggerating, Mr. Rossi." She smiled, a little embarrassed at his praise.

The mayor began to ask more about the hotel. Angelina stood alongside John, feeling special that he wanted her there with him, that he was pleased with her work. Was he impressed enough to make her a Rossi International employee? If it were possible for her to land a management position when the Grand Haven opened, life could be nearly perfect. Her pulse began to pound with optimism.

"Sorry I'm late," a breathless Valerie Peters said as she walked up to the group.

John smiled, taking her arm. "Valerie, I'm so glad you could make it." He turned toward the crowd. "Everyone, I'd like you to meet Valerie Peters. She's the interior designer for the hotel."

Angelina watched as the attractive woman shook hands with everyone. The men seemed grateful she'd joined the party. She was dressed in a slinky black dress that made Angelina feel like Mary Poppins. Worse, Valerie had latched on to John, letting everyone know that they were more than working acquaintances. Maybe they were a couple back in New York.

By the time the buffet was served, Angelina had found her way to the kitchen and seated herself in the corner as the caterers worked around her. Everyone had pretty much paired off into couples. Tuck was nowhere in sight, but she didn't expect him to be. They were just friends. He was doing her a favor by bringing her. But it was awful being alone all the time. Especially in a crowd.

Shelby came into the kitchen. "What are you doing in here?"

"I got tired of the crowd," Angelina lied. How could she explain that she didn't fit in?

Her sister-in-law raised an eyebrow. "Or maybe just of a certain blonde?"

Angelina wished everyone would just stop messing in her life. "Look, John Rossi can be with anyone he wants."

"Fine. But you can't hide out here all night." Shelby put her hands on her hips. "Jeez, Lina. You're a Covelli, get back in there and pitch yourself. Act like the professional businesswoman you want to be." She turned and marched out.

A little shocked at her sister-in-law's words, Angelina realized she *was* hiding out. And she didn't want to do anything to spoil the party. Shelby had put too much into this night. During a quick trip to the bathroom, Angelina freshened her makeup, then headed back toward the front of the house.

She began mingling again. It wasn't hard at all. She knew most of the people, either from business, church or just from living in Haven Springs all her life.

The next hour passed quickly. But all the time Angelina could feel John's presence, hear his laughter. When she finally got the nerve to look at him, she discovered that he was watching her, too. Heat spread to her stomach as his gaze refused to let her go. Then Valerie showed up at his side.

A dull pain gripped Angelina's chest as she turned away. She wanted to go home.

An arm came across her shoulders. "Where have you been all night?"

Angelina looked up at Tuck. "I'm sorry. Did you

miss me?'' She slipped her arm around his waist and leaned into him.

''Yes, but you seemed busy with business,'' Tuck said with laughter in his voice.

''That's about it. A lot of business.''

''Isn't that what you wanted? To make more connections?'' he asked.

''Sure. In fact, I got a job prospect similar to what I'm doing now.''

''Isn't that good?'' he asked.

She shrugged. ''I had something a little different in mind.''

Tuck leaned closer. ''Like maybe working for Rossi?''

''It's a big company,'' she said. ''There's a lot of chance for advancement.''

''Among other things.'' His grin was wicked. ''I may be a little slow on the uptake sometimes, but I saw your eyes light up the minute you saw him.''

When she tried to turn away, Tuck cupped her chin with his palm and made her look at him. ''You're going to deny it?''

''Yes, anything other than a business relationship with John Rossi would be disastrous.''

''Why not take a chance at discovering something special happening between the two of you?''

Angelina shook her head. ''No. Nothing's going to happen.''

Tuck moved closer. ''I bet if I kissed you, he would come over here and rip my head off. Or we could just leave and let him think we're having a hot rendezvous.''

Angelina smiled at the crazy notion, then looked up to catch sight of a pretty brunette by the door. ''I think you might be the one who wants to ditch me. Who's the attractive woman looking daggers at me?"

He grinned. "Sally Parsons. She's a new teacher at the high school. I'm hopin' she'll teach me a thing or two." Tuck winked at Angelina.

"So what are you doing here with me? Go. I'm going to stay and help Shelby anyway." Before she could push Tuck away, he planted a quick, sweet kiss on her lips. When he pulled back, he smiled.

Shocked, Angelina couldn't speak. Tuck leaned down to whisper in her ear, "That was strictly for me. Thanks for the nice evening. I'm just going to run Sally home and I'll be back to help with the cleanup. Try to stay out of trouble till then."

She watched as Tuck left and found her party mood slowly fading. She needed some fresh air. Wandering through the crowded rooms she ended up in the kitchen again, then grabbed a tablecloth off the counter and went out the back door.

Dim lights circled the bare patio, now devoid of the lawn furniture which had been put away for the winter. A cold breeze lifted Angelina's hair as she shivered and quickly wrapped the cloth around her. She rubbed her arms, trying to bring some warmth to her skin. Darned if she was going back inside. Heading down the path through Miss Hannah's rose garden, she stopped in the middle of the bare bushes. No more roses this year, she thought, just a long, frigid winter to look forward to.

Angelina had disappeared. John looked around the room, but couldn't see her anywhere. He knew that she hadn't left with Tucker. After witnessing the kiss the cowboy had planted on her, John wondered how in the hell the man could leave with another woman.

Needing to see that she was okay, John excused himself from the group of guests and began his search. He explored each room until he ended up in the kitchen talking with one of the waiters who told him she'd gone outside.

Relieved, he headed for the seemingly deserted patio. The cold air hit him, but he ignored it, continuing his journey along the flagstone path to the garden where he found Angelina. She made an exquisite picture standing in the moonlight. Her hair was like ebony satin where the soft curls lay on her delicate shoulders. His palms itched to run his fingers through the long strands. His gaze roamed over her oval face with its wide-set eyes and the full luscious mouth that made him hungry for a taste. He moved down to the tempting dress that fitted her shapely body to perfection. She had taken his breath away and stirred his desire. All evening he'd kept telling himself to stay away, but he couldn't. She drew him like a magnet.

"Aren't you cold?" he asked. He hadn't been anywhere near cold since he'd walked in the door tonight and seen her.

Angelina swung around. "John! What are you doing out here?"

He walked closer. "I needed some fresh air." He took off his jacket and placed it over her shoulders. "You're shivering."

"I'm okay." She shrugged off the coat and tried to hand it back to him.

"Stubborn," he murmured. He took it from her and again put it across her shoulders, catching the soft fragrance that was purely Angelina. "You can't stay out here dressed in that." He looked down at the white tablecloth she was using as a shawl. He knew that underneath, her shoulders were bare. "You'll freeze."

"What about you?"

"Don't worry about me. I was getting too warm inside." Hell, he'd been burning up watching her walk around in her sexy dress.

"Fine. Thanks." She accepted the jacket, then continued down the path, disappearing into the shadows of the trees.

He went after her. "Hey, where are you headed in the dark?"

"Just walking."

He looked around the yard, at the big maple trees and trimmed shrubs along the property. "It's pretty out here. I bet the rose garden is something when it's in bloom." He suddenly felt as awkward as a teenager. Angelina had that effect on him. "My grandmother Lia had a rose garden in Italy. When I was little I would go out with her and she would show me how to care for them." That was long before she left his grandfather, he thought.

Angelina sighed. "I think all grandmothers must have rose gardens. Nonna Vittoria spends hours in hers. I'm glad she has a lot of interests to keep her busy." She stopped when they came to a white building that resembled a cottage.

"What's this place?"

She stepped up on the small porch, went to the mailbox and took something out. A key. She unlocked the door. "At one time it was a gardener's cottage. Rafe fixed it up and now it's Shelby's retreat. She's a writer, you know."

They stepped inside and Angelina turned on a small

lamp by the door. He looked at her and had to slip his hands into his trouser pockets to keep from touching her. "No, I didn't know." He shrugged. "But there's a lot I don't know."

Angelina finally smiled, setting her face aglow in the dim light. "That's a first, a man admitting he doesn't know everything."

He stepped closer, watching her eyes grow wide. He raised a hand and caressed her cheek. "I know you take my breath away just by looking at me." He lifted her chin with his fingertip and stared into her eyes.

"You shouldn't say that," she whispered.

"I'm only speaking the truth."

She stiffened. "What about Ms. Peters?"

He tried to hide his smile. "I prefer eyes blue as the ocean and hair as black as midnight."

Dio, he couldn't help himself. He bent his head and when she didn't stop him, his mouth caressed hers gently. She sucked in a breath as he pulled away, then he went back for another taste. The jacket and cloth she wore silently dropped to the floor, unnoticed. "Since that first kiss, I've wanted more. I can't seem to stop myself with you."

"Oh, John," she whispered as her eyes drifted shut.

This time one of his hands went to her hair, pulling her close, making the mating of their mouths more intimate. His other hand circled her waist and drew her against him, pressing every inch of her body against his.

Angelina's hands left a heated trail up his chest, then her long fingers tangled in his hair. She made a soft whimpering sound and leaned into him. He groaned and pushed his tongue into her mouth, tasting her, unable to get enough of her. But he wouldn't mind in the least spending forever trying.

Angelina's knees were weak when John tore his mouth from hers, but he continued to rain kisses along her neck, then across her chest. "You are so beautiful, *cara.*" Each word was emphasized by another kiss, raising goosebumps along her skin, and an awareness that she'd never known before.

His hands moved to the straps on her gown as his dark eyes locked with hers. She trembled in anticipation, and finally his hands lowered the straps and cool air touched her bare skin, followed by his warm mouth. She gasped from the pleasure of the new sensations. She knew she should stop him. But she didn't have the strength. And in her heart she didn't want to.

Outside there were voices and laughter that tore her from her fantasy.

"John..." She tried to pull away, but he held her.

"Shh, *cara.*" He soothed her with his voice, then released her as she fixed her dress. Embarrassed, Angelina could only think about getting away. How could she face this man again?

John knew he'd gone too far. He never should have looked for her. "I'm sorry, Angelina. I can't seem to resist you."

She jerked around. "We have to resist, John. We work together."

"What is wrong with us sharing time together while I'm in town?"

She marched around the small area of the combination living room and kitchenette. "Because it isn't right."

"What have we done that's so wrong?"

"Nothing, and we should keep it that way."

He nodded. ‘‘I guess so.’’

‘‘I mean…I'll never see you again. Except when the hotel opens. I read that you go to all your openings.’’

He was surprised she knew. ‘‘Where did you find that out?’’

She shrugged. ‘‘I did research. It's something I do when I'm looking for a job.’’

‘‘Job? But you have a job.’’

‘‘But not my independence. Working at Covelli and Sons has been the only job I've ever had. Since high school, I've worked in the office. I planned to strike out on my own after college, but then there was my dad's accident. Everyone needed to hang together. Then other things stopped me. Don't get me wrong. I wanted to help out. But it's been over three years now, and its past time I was out on my own.’’ She raised her head and their eyes met. ‘‘That's one of the reasons I felt we shouldn't get involved. I want to work for you—for Rossi International.’’

John was stunned. The familiar hurt struck him like a piercing blow. This was a replay of his failed relationship with Selina. No one wanted him just for what *he* could give them. Angelina Covelli was no different. He should have never forgotten his reason for coming here. Never forgotten how much damage the Covellis had done to his grandfather. Well, Angelina had just reminded him. ‘‘What can you offer me?’’ he asked coldly.

She swallowed. ‘‘I know I would be an excellent person to work at the Grand Haven. When the hotel opens, of course. I know the area and the people.’’

‘‘It takes a hell of a lot more than that to run a hotel.’’

She stiffened. ‘‘I'm willing to learn. I'm great with

computers. I have a bachelor's degree in Business Administration with a minor in Computer Science. I feel with some training I could be a valued employee, Mr. Rossi."

How in the hell had this turned into a job interview? "Mr. Rossi," he said as he cupped her stubborn chin. "Minutes ago, *cara,* you were crying out my name in pleasure."

She pulled away. "I didn't mean for that to happen. It was wrong. But I don't want it to stop you from considering me as a potential employee."

Hell, that was the *last* way he'd been thinking about her. Resentment overwhelmed him, but he wasn't ready to walk away from the beautiful Angelina Covelli. If she wanted to use him, he could return the favor. Just how far would she go for a job?

"Monday morning I'm flying up to our Stratton Mountain resort in Vermont for a few days." It was supposed to be his downtime, a mini vacation. Why not take along a beautiful diversion? "The snow season hasn't officially started yet, so I go to kick back. You're welcome to come along."

"Really? You're giving me a chance? Will this be considered training for a position?"

John shook his head. "I didn't say anything about training. I'm inviting you to go—with me."

The air seemed to be trapped in her lungs as Angelina stared at him. How dare he! "I won't sleep with you to get a job."

He gave her a hint of a smile. "No one asked you to. I thought you'd like to come with me and see our hotel. But this is my recuperation time. I don't want to think about work. I don't have a problem with you looking around to see how a hotel is run. It's your choice.'' He turned and walked out of the cottage.

And Angelina was left to make the biggest decision of her life.

Chapter Eight

"I'm going to Vermont and you can't stop me," Angelina called to Rafe from her bedroom door. Then she turned back to her packing, hoping that was the last of her brother's meddling.

It wasn't. Too soon she heard the returning footsteps.

Rafe marched into her room, an angry scowl on his face. "I forbid you."

She glanced over her shoulder. "You're kidding, right?"

"No, I'm not." His expression softened. "Look, Lina. This isn't a good idea. Something could happen...."

No one needed to tell Angelina that. She'd spent the past twenty-four hours asking herself if she were crazy for taking this chance. That was it. She'd never taken any chances, and although going to Vermont terrified her, it might be her one chance—her only chance to break away.

"I hope something *does* happen," she said. "I hope

I can prove to John Rossi I'm good enough to work for his company."

Rafe crossed his arms over his chest, trying to look large and intimidating. More and more he looked like their father.

"You really think that Rossi has anything else on his mind besides getting you into the sack?"

His blunt words made her blink, and, surprisingly, thrilled her. "I'm a big girl, Rafe. I can handle myself." She refused to back down. "I'm not going to let anything happen that I don't want to happen."

"See! That's just what I'm talking about." He ran his hands over his face as he began to pace. "No. No. I can't let you go."

Surprisingly, Angelina remained calm. "You have no say in whether I go or not. I didn't tell you how to behave when you began your relationship with Shelby."

"So, you're admitting that something is going on between you and John."

She zipped up her bag and looked around for her tote and purse, hoping she didn't have the guilty look that Rafe knew so well. "I'm not admitting anything. I'm an adult and what I do is my business."

He took hold of her arm. "Look, Lina, I'm only trying to protect you. I know when you lost Justin how badly you..." He released her. "No, I have no idea what it was like." His dark eyes held such love. "But I saw the pain you went through, and I couldn't do a thing to help you."

She swallowed back the tightness in her throat and touched his cheek. "You were there for me."

"Then let me be there now. Rossi is way out of your

league. Besides, he'll be gone soon and you'll be nothing but a memory of a pleasant weekend."

That hurt. "I'm not going to be anyone's memory, pleasant or otherwise. I'm going to check out another Rossi hotel. I want to see how it's run, so I know what is expected of me when I become manager of the Grand Haven."

"Damn it, Lina, just don't fall in love with the guy."

She glanced away. Could she love someone like John Rossi? He was nothing like Justin. Her sweet, loving Justin. "I only loved one guy." That was all she needed to say.

He nodded.

"I love you, Rafe, for wanting to take care of me. But I'm not a child. I'm twenty-four, nearly twenty-five."

His expression softened. "But I promised Dad I would..."

"Then be there for me." She took a breath. "Don't try and stop me from wanting to be independent."

He put his arms around her. "But you're my sister. How can I stop watching out for you, wanting to take care of you?"

Angelina smiled, then kissed him. "Have a baby of your own."

Suddenly Rafe's face flushed and he glanced away.

"Oh, my gosh, Shelby's pregnant."

He started to speak, then finally nodded with a big grin. "Yeah, she is. But you've got to keep it quiet for a while. She's not even six weeks yet."

"Oh, that's wonderful," she said, then realized again that her brothers had moved on with their lives. It was time for her to take a stab at hers. "You should be with Shelby."

"I'm taking care of her just fine."

Angelina crossed her arms. "I bet she doesn't know you're here."

"Yes, she does. I told her I was coming by to see you off."

"Then kiss me goodbye and go home."

Rafe hugged her. "I love you, sis. I just don't want you to get hurt."

Angelina was touched. "It's part of growing up, Rafe. Just give me your blessing and tell me you trust me to make my own decisions."

"Of course I do. Just know that you can call if you need anything. Even if it's just to talk."

She nodded. "Now, if I don't get a move on John's going to leave without me. Carry my suitcases downstairs."

Rafe lifted her two bags and started down the hall. Angelina brushed at her navy wool slacks and white sweater, then slipped on her wine-colored blazer.

Her heart racing with excitement, she made her way downstairs and saw John waiting for her. He was dressed in dark brown trousers and a sand-colored polo shirt with a tan suede jacket. He smiled and she couldn't seem to manage to breathe.

"Ready?"

No, she wanted to scream, but instead she nodded. Her mother and Nonna walked into the room. Maria and her daughter had had a long discussion last night, and her mother had finally relented to the trip admitting that her daughter had a right to make her own decisions. They hugged each other. "You be careful, Lina."

"I will, Mom."

Nonna hugged Angelina, but didn't say anything.

She had come into her granddaughter's room last night and they had talked. Strangely they'd ended up discussing Nonna falling in love with their grandfather, Enrico.

"I'll phone when I arrive," Angelina promised, then caught her brother talking with John. Oh, no. She had to save him.

"We should go," she said.

A little over an hour later, they boarded Rossi International's private jet.

It all was happening so fast, Angelina thought as she took the seat across from John in the plane. She belted herself in while John gave instructions to the pilot. Excitement raced through her as the plane began to taxi.

She hadn't traveled much in her life. Now she was jetting to Vermont for a few days, then, on the return trip, stopping in New York.

John watched Angelina's eyes grow large as the jet lifted off the ground. If she were frightened, she hadn't let on, but he doubted Angelina Covelli would willingly show any weakness. He also doubted she had ever passed on a dare, either. That was one of the things he liked about her. She didn't give in easily. No doubt a trait she'd inherited from her grandmother. His thoughts went to his grandfather in Italy. He knew nothing about his grandson meeting the Covellis, much less awarding them a contract to work for him.

Once again, John was reminded of how foolish he was to invite Angelina to go with him. Not only had he broken his cardinal rule by getting involved with a co-worker, but he was taking Angelina to his private getaway. The one place where he'd always gone—alone.

Now, Angelina was going to be at his side for a few

days without her family or job to hide behind. Even knowing that she'd planned on using him, he still wanted her. He could easily turn the tables on her—make her want him. If he spent time with her, shared her bed, then he might be able to get her out of his system.

The jet leveled off and he saw the concern in Angelina's blue eyes. He leaned forward and took hold of her hands. They were cold and clammy to the touch. She didn't resist as he quickly wrapped them between his.

They were slender, her palms soft, her fingers long and tapered. He couldn't help but wonder how they would feel on his skin. Warmth surged through him, settling deep in his gut as he looked up to see her eyes turn dark with desire.

He released her hands and moved back in his seat. "The pilot says it's clear skies all the way to Vermont. So it should be a pretty smooth ride."

"I'm a novice at this."

He bet she was a novice at other things, too.

When she leaned toward the window, his gaze caught her slender waist, the outline of her full breasts in her fitted sweater. "It's so beautiful up here." She looked back at him, her eyes aglow. "You're so lucky to get to travel everywhere."

He pursed his lips. "I have been to a few interesting places." It had gotten old fast. After being in Haven Springs this past month, he found he envied the simplicity the Covellis had in their day-to-day living.

His attention fell again on Angelina. Too bad he would never fit in there.

The plane landed in Hartford, Connecticut, and they were met in front of the terminal by an employee standing by a four-wheel-drive vehicle with Rossi Mountain Inn displayed on the side.

"Angelina, I want you to meet Todd McCall. He works at the inn as one of the managers."

The golden-haired man smiled. "It's nice to meet you, Angelina."

Todd was about her age. He stood nearly six feet tall with a long lanky frame. His eyes were a gentle gray and his smile ready. "I'm actually a ski bum, with a degree in hotel management. Working up here has great benefits. I'm also the local ski instructor. Do you ski?"

"Some," she said. "Mostly cross-country."

"Well, if you need any help just give me a holler," Todd offered, then looked at John. "On second thought, I bet John could show you everything you need to know."

Angelina saw John's intense look. "I'm hoping while I'm here I'm able to see how the operation is run," she said.

Todd and John exchanged a look, then finally Todd spoke, "If I can help in any way, just let me know."

"I've already talked with Shannon," John said. "She's going to clear some time for Angelina tomorrow."

Angelina looked curiously at John. Had he really done that for her? She wanted to thank him, but couldn't help but wonder what it was going to cost her.

Todd loaded the bags in the back of the car, opened the car door and Angelina climbed in. John took the front seat and spent half of the two-hour trip to the lodge discussing hotel business with Todd, then the other half talking on his cell phone. Angelina sat in the backseat not minding the quiet time to view the scenery.

Although the countryside was beautiful and intriguing to look at, with the evergreen trees lightly dusted with snow, she was thinking about how she and John would be spending the next four days together. With no family around, she was on her own. The thought excited her, but also terrified her. Deep down she knew she was playing with fire, and she could definitely get burned.

She sucked in a breath at the thought of John's kiss. The feelings he'd managed to unearth in her. She'd forgotten her common sense in the cottage Friday night. And she couldn't let that happen again. Even if John was out to seduce her, she had to focus on business. Drawing a long breath, she tried to think how she planned to protect her heart.

Todd turned off the main highway and drove along a two-lane road for another ten minutes. They traveled through thick rows of pine trees until they reached the base of the mountains where a three-story lodge came into view. The rich sunny-gold-hued building with emerald-green trim stood out from the mountainside with a black roof that arched high toward the sky. The majestic mountain range created a breathtaking backdrop with its light blanket of fresh snow.

Their car pulled into the circular drive and stopped under the canvas awning at the double doors. A bellman came out to greet them.

"Good afternoon, Mr. Rossi," the young man said. "It's nice to have you back."

"It's good to be back, Sam," John said as he helped Angelina out of the car. "Please take my luggage to my suite. And take Ms. Covelli's to the adjoining Milano Suite."

"Yes, sir." The bellman started off.

A private *adjoining* suite. A warning bell went off in Angelina's head. She didn't have to be hit over the head to know what John had in mind.

"No!" she called. When the man stopped and looked at her, she turned to John. "I mean, do I *really* need a suite?"

John remained silent for a while, then pulled her aside. "There are no ordinary rooms at the inn. They're all suites."

Angelina looked into his mesmerizing brown eyes. "Oh. But I just don't want people here to think that there...there is something going on between us."

His mouth twitched. "Isn't there?"

"No," she insisted.

"That's not what your kisses said."

"And that was a mistake. I told you, I want to learn the business—that's all."

His eyes suddenly turned dark and cold. "And I repeat all the rooms in the inn are suites. And these happen to adjoin—with a locked door between them. It's these rooms, or Todd can take you back to the airport."

She would give anything to tell the cocky Mr. Rossi she was leaving, but she'd probably never have this opportunity to see the inner workings of a successful hotel again. "All right, I'll stay."

"Sam, take the luggage up," he said, then he took her arm and walked her through the front door into a large open lobby filled with huge potted plants. The atmosphere wasn't typical ski lodge. The thick green carpeting felt luxurious under her feet. A row of windows showed off the spectacular view. The inn had more of a Mediterranean look with its decor and dark furnishings.

They approached the elevators and John pressed the button. The ride up was silent except for the pounding of her heart in her ears. When they reached the fourth floor, John took her arm and they walked down the wide hall to the door at the end.

"This is my suite." Then he stepped down the hall to another door. When the bellman appeared with their luggage, John took a key from Sam.

John watched Angelina's eyes widen. "This is for you," he said, wishing he could wipe that terrified look off her face. "Don't worry, I won't intrude on your privacy. Whoever you invite inside your suite is up to you." He raised her hand and placed a soft kiss against her palm. "I hope you will have dinner with me tonight. Downstairs, or if you're too tired from the trip, I can have room service sent up."

She licked her lips and he felt weak at the innocent action. Or was it innocent? Damn. She had him crazy. Most of the time all he wanted to do was touch her, kiss her, feel her sweet surrender as she gave in to his will.

"No, I'd like to have dinner with you."

Her simple acceptance thrilled him. "Good. You rest now. I'll see you downstairs at seven."

She nodded, and handed her key to Sam. The bellman unlocked her door, took her suitcases into her suite, then stepped back into the hallway. Angelina entered her room and closed the door.

John entered his familiar suite and sat on the bed. He looked at the wall that separated him from Angelina. He had to keep reminding himself that Angelina was trying to use him. She did not care about him—

only what he could do for her. And he didn't tolerate abuse—from anyone.

That's right. Stay good and mad at her, then you won't want to kiss her every time she flashes those big blue eyes.

Hell, he only wanted a relaxing weekend with a beautiful woman. Then he would have her out of his system and could move on and leave her and the Covelli family behind.

Three hours later, rested from the trip, Angelina changed into a red sweater tucked into a long charcoal skirt, and rode the elevator down to the lobby. She walked across the lobby to the front desk.

"Hi, I'm Angelina Covelli, and I'm to meet Mr. Rossi. Can you direct me to the restaurant?"

The woman was about thirty and had a friendly smile. "So nice to meet you, Angelina," she said. "I'm Shannon Keely, the inn's manager. John said you were going to be with us for a few days, and that you wanted a tour."

"I hope you don't mind."

"Of course not. I love showing off the inn." Shannon looked at the twenty-something clerk. "I'll be right back, Jace." She came around the desk, then led Angelina across the lobby toward the back of the hotel. "We're in a slow spot now. The big rush will start on the weekend. We're expecting another snowstorm in the next twenty-four hours."

They came to an arched doorway. Printed across the top was the name, *Per Amore.* For Love. Angelina couldn't help but wonder if John Rossi had chosen the name.

They were met by a hostess, Cindy. After the introductions, Shannon left and Cindy escorted Angelina through the nearly deserted restaurant. A soft romantic ballad filled the dark, intimate room, and each table was covered with a starched white cloth topped by a flickering candle. A perfect place for a seduction, Angelina thought as they arrived at a corner table where John waited.

He was wearing black trousers and a slate-gray sweater. "I see you made it." He stood up and helped Angelina with her chair. "Thank you, Cindy."

After the hostess left, John returned to his seat and reached for a bottle of white wine chilling next to the table. "Would you care for some, or would you rather wait until dinner?"

Hoping it would help with her nervousness, she nodded. "I'll have a glass now, thank you."

He poured the wine into a crystal glass and she took a slow sip. A dry but pleasant taste filled her mouth. "This is delicious."

"I thought you might like it. It's from a small Italian winery. We use their wines and champagnes exclusively. It's our goal to make everything as pleasurable as possible for our guests." He raised a dark eyebrow. "That brings them back for more. Don't you agree, Angelina?"

Angelina couldn't concentrate on his words, she was too busy being captivated by his voice, his eyes.

She shook her head and cleared her dry throat. "Of course."

"That's also my goal for the Grand Haven Hotel. Not just to attract local people, but to draw an elite crowd that wants something unique in a hotel."

"You've done very well here. It's beautiful. But it's not as large as I expected."

"This is a hideaway, Angelina. Our guests come here to get away from the feeling of being crowded. We only have fifty-five guest suites."

She took another sip of wine. "How can you make any money?"

He smiled and her stomach suddenly felt tight. "At the prices our guests are willing to pay, we do rather nicely."

"Oh." She took a deep breath. "Do you get many families here?"

He shook his head. "Not many. But we do have a few cottages for families along with baby-sitting services if needed."

"Is that so they'll be seen and not heard?" She finished the last of her wine and watched as John refilled her glass.

"That's so their parents can have some uninterrupted time together."

"Oh, my. John Rossi believes in romance."

He gave her a wounded look. "What made you think I didn't believe in romance?"

She took another drink, studying the sexy man across from her. "You told me so when you were moving into the apartment."

"I told you that I didn't believe in long-term relationships. I definitely believe in romance. In fact, what I've been imagining with you is very romantic."

She drew in a breath. "Please, John. Remember our agreement. This is business."

"I only agreed to refrain from doing anything you don't want me to." He smiled knowingly, as if he had gained the upper hand.

Well, he was wrong. She was going to work for the man, nothing more.

They ordered dinner and spent the next hour talking about their personal lives. John asked her questions about her family, but she discovered that every time she inquired about his family, he quickly changed the subject. However, by the end of the evening, Angelina had managed to get him to agree to her spending the morning with Shannon. In exchange, she would go skiing with him in the afternoon.

After a third glass of wine and eating far too much delicious food, Angelina finally called an end to the evening.

John thanked the chef and escorted her upstairs. After they got on the elevator, she smiled, then found the urge to giggle. She let go of a little laugh.

"What's so funny?" John asked.

She shook her head. "Sorry."

"No, I apologize. I thought you could handle a little wine."

She stiffened. "I can handle my wine just fine."

"Sorry. I guess it's probably jet lag." He took her by the arm when the elevator doors opened.

"That's it," she agreed. "Jet lag. I'm tired, too."

John chuckled as they made their way down the dimly lit hall to her room. "Where's your key?" He held out his hand.

She searched her purse, then realized that she'd left it on her dresser. "It's in my room."

Without a comment, John went to the door of his suite. "I should be able to open the adjoining door with my key," he said as he led her into his room. Angelina stood in the entry of the large suite, leading to a huge sitting room decorated in cinnamon and forest-green. A stone fireplace was ready to be lit with extra wood neatly stacked next to the hearth. A row of windows showed the view of the twinkling lights outside. Her suite was lovely, but this was incredible.

John stood at the door which led directly into her room jiggling the handle. "It's not working." He walked over to the table by the bed and called down to the front desk. After he hung up, he came to her.

"Someone will be up in a few minutes."

"I'll go wait outside."

He reached for her to stop her departure. "You aren't going to stand outside in the hall."

Angelina tried to move away, but he refused to let her go. Her breathing grew rapid as it mingled with John's. "But how will they find me?" she asked.

"I told them you were in my room. I'm sorry if I gave you too much wine."

"No, you didn't," she denied. "I'm just glad you gave me this chance to come here. How will I thank you?" As soon as the words were out, she wanted to take them back.

In answer John tugged her into his arms, allowing her to inhale his familiar scent. His touch was so strong, yet gentle, making her feel secure.

No, she couldn't let this happen. She pulled back and looked up at his face. His dark eyes were so mesmerizing. "I've got to go." If she didn't make her escape now, she'd weaken and give him anything he asked for. "'Night, John." She had started to turn away when he reached for her again.

"Not so fast," he said bringing her back into his arms. "If I'm not going to see you tomorrow morning, I'll need something to sustain me."

His mouth closed over hers in a slow lingering kiss. Without giving herself time to call on her common sense, Angelina allowed him to work his magic on her.

She loved the feel of this man's arms around her, of being cradled against his strong body. He pulled away from her lips and looked at her, his eyes glowing with an inner fire. There was no doubt, he wanted her.

When his head dipped again, she had a little courage left to fight him. "John...we shouldn't."

"It was perfectly all right a few moments ago."

The kiss *had* been perfect. And that fact had her more angry with herself than with him for allowing him to get so close. "I think it would be best if I...we keep our distance," she said, nearly choking on her words.

His eyes flashed with a sudden anger. "Fine, if that's what you want. I usually don't have to beg women to spend time with me." He released her. "I am on vacation. I'm capable of finding plenty to keep me occupied."

She nodded. Why did the whole idea make her sad? "This is for the best, John. You'll be returning to New York..." You'll forget all about me, she added silently.

He jammed his hands into his pockets. "Yes. New York. I have been gone a while. There are friends I've neglected and engagements coming up."

She really didn't want to hear this. But it was the right thing, she told herself. No involvement. That way no one gets hurt.

There was a soft knock on the door. "That's my key," she said, and began slowly moving away. "Thank you for dinner, John. Good night."

At the door she bravely looked back. Her eyes met his and she suddenly ached to rush into his arms.

He stepped forward, then stopped. "Good night, *cara.*"

She rushed out and once in the safety of her suite she turned the dead bolt. She could keep John Rossi out of her rooms but nothing would keep him out of her dreams.

Chapter Nine

At eight o'clock the next morning, John stood on his private balcony overlooking the mountain range. It had snowed last night, leaving three inches of fresh powder on the ski slopes.

He took a sip of coffee from his mug. "Just perfect," he murmured, still drowsy. He'd never gone to sleep, thanks to the recurring thoughts of the heated kiss he had shared with Angelina.

With a groan, he leaned against the railing. Although he'd had a fleeting thought of seducing her for using him to get a job, she somehow had turned the tables on him.

The call he'd gotten thirty minutes ago from Shannon informed him that not only was the lodge booked for the weekend, but Angelina had been working at the front desk all morning. His manager had also tossed in that Angelina was a quick study and had picked up the hotel's computer system without any problem.

Just perfect.

Damn, how did this get so complicated? All he'd intended to do was renovate the Grand Haven Hotel. His mistakes had been his curiosity over a fifty-year-old curse and getting involved with the Covelli family. With Angelina. Hadn't he learned from his past history with women?

Guess not. Since the first moment he'd seen Angelina Covelli, he hadn't been thinking with his head. He couldn't stop wanting her in his bed. And why not have her? Wasn't she using him in much the same way?

He knew it was senseless, but he wanted her to come to him for reasons other than a job. But when she discovered his true identity, she wasn't going to come to him at all—except maybe to slap his face.

He rubbed a hand across his cheek as if feeling the sting already. "Oh, Nonno Giovanni. How did I get into this mess?"

John wasn't going to delve into his feelings. That was a place he didn't go anymore. Simply, he was physically attracted to Angelina, and wanted to spend time with her. Nothing more. By the end of the week, she'd be back in Indiana, and he'd return to New York. He hoped they'd both have fond memories of their time in Vermont.

Returning inside, he pulled off his robe, tossed it on the bed and went into the bathroom. The only way he could relax was to make himself scarce. He turned on the faucet in the shower, then stepped inside and shivered as the cold spray hit his body. After a few agonizing minutes, he toweled off and returned to the bedroom, then dressed in a red sweater and a pair of ski pants.

He decided he was going to ski this morning and work off some excess energy. Maybe he'd sleep better tonight. Although, he doubted anything would keep his thoughts from Angelina.

It was going to be a long three days.

"Welcome to the Rossi Mountain Inn, Mr. Collinsworth," Angelina said with a bright smile. "We have your suite all ready."

A gentleman in his fifties, gray at the temples, smiled at her. "Hello…" he squinted at her name tag, "…Angelina."

"This is your first visit to our inn?" He nodded as she took his platinum credit card and ran it through the machine, like she'd seen Shannon do all morning, then handed it back to him. "We want to make sure that you have everything you need."

"Well, thank you," he said. "But I can't think of anything right now."

"I hope you'll be taking advantage of the fresh blanket of snow on the slopes. Will Mrs. Collinsworth be joining you?"

"She'll be arriving tomorrow. It's our anniversary."

Angelina smiled. "So, a weekend away with just the two of you. How romantic. May I suggest several activities? There's cross-country skiing, or we have sleigh rides all afternoon until nightfall. There's a van that can take you around to many of the sights in the area, such as our famous covered bridges, and in Bennington there's a battle monument that is the largest in the country."

"I wasn't planning on wandering that far from the hotel."

Angelina thought for a moment. "Well, there's plenty to do close by, too. Treat yourself to our spa facilities and our heated pool." She smiled. "I bet your wife would love to be pampered for a few hours. We also have a small theater and tomorrow they're showing the movie classic, *Casablanca.*"

Angelina saw the man's eyes light up as she went on. "And you can top it off with a wonderful candlelight dinner in the dining room, or if you prefer, in your suite. Our chef has created a delicious *tagliarini all'aragosta,* made with Maine lobster," she continued, "and an almond sponge cake served with mascarpone sauce."

"I think you've given me some good ideas," he said. "Could you make a reservation for two in the dining room for tomorrow evening? A nice quiet table."

"It would be my pleasure." Angelina nodded. "How about a bouquet of flowers?"

"That would be nice."

"I'll arrange for a dozen long-stemmed roses to be delivered tomorrow evening about five."

"Oh, my wife would love that. Thank you, Angelina."

"It will be my pleasure, Mr. Collinsworth," she said again, as she handed him the key to his room, then motioned for Sam to take his bags upstairs.

"You did a wonderful job," Shannon said as she came up behind Angelina. "Mr. Collinsworth came here for a special occasion, and you helped him make their stay even more memorable. Oh, his wife is going to be thrilled."

"I just watched you. It really comes naturally for me and it's so much fun." Excited, Angelina picked up the phone and called the inn's florist to place the rose order. Then she called *Per Amore* to reserve a secluded table for two for the next night. She even alerted the vocalist at the piano bar to watch for them so he could sing a special song for the couple.

She hung up the phone with a sigh. "That's done. Mrs. Collinsworth is going to be so surprised."

Shannon leaned against the counter. "It must be nice to have someone who's been committed to you for so many years," she said. "I haven't had a relationship that lasted longer than my eighteen-month marriage. My husband resented the time I spent in my job."

"That's not fair," Angelina said. "You have a right to a career."

"You mean you wouldn't give up everything for that special man?"

Angelina glanced away, not wanting to go into her personal life. "There isn't a special man in my life. Since I'm single, I'm looking forward to a long, successful career. So far, I've only worked for my family's business. And over the years, my brothers have been pretty protective. It's time for me to strike out on my own. That's why I'm here. I'm hoping to get a job at Rossi International."

Shannon leaned closer. "And these brothers of yours let you fly off in a private jet with John Rossi?"

Angelina blushed. "I convinced them that there's nothing personal between us."

Shannon looked toward the front door. "You better tell John then."

Angelina drew a shaky breath at the sight of John standing at the main entrance. He was talking with Sam, but his gaze was on her. His dark eyes were compelling, drawing her in, making her want what she knew she couldn't have. But making her want it just the same.

John was a handsome man, but he had something

more than looks. There was an air of confidence about him. She bet he was a powerhouse in the boardroom...and in the bedroom. All at once heat rose to her face and she glanced away. What was she thinking? She'd made her choice.

A sudden emptiness surrounded her as she wondered if she would always feel this way. She'd had love once, knew how it felt to care so much about another person that nothing else mattered. And she knew how much it hurt when it fell apart. She would never risk her heart again.

That afternoon, John insisted Angelina see some of the countryside. More snow was due that night which was wonderful for skiers, but made it hard to get around. John had one of the horse-drawn sleighs waiting outside the main entrance when she came down.

"I hope you're dressed warmly enough," he said escorting her to the sleigh.

"I'm wearing long johns," she said as she climbed in and sat down on the cushioned seat. He followed her, then covered their legs with a wool blanket.

The driver took the reins and called a command to the pair of Morgan horses. The sleigh jerked forward and soon was gliding smoothly over the snowy trail.

Angelina was enthralled with the scenery. The sun was going down behind the mountain, casting shadows over the pristine snow. Pine trees were heavy with white powder, the branches hanging low to the ground. Off in the distance, Angelina saw two deer.

"Oh, look," she said. "Aren't they beautiful?"

"One of the many advantages of being out in the wilderness. I don't get to see much of that in New York City."

Angelina looked at him. "We get some out at the lake. But with more development, we're losing more of the beautiful creatures."

"I guess you have to give up some things for progress," he said. "And speaking of progress, Shannon said you did a wonderful job behind the desk."

John was seated close beside her. Saying he made Angelina nervous was an understatement. "Shannon's been a wonderful teacher. I just followed her lead."

Their eyes locked. She couldn't even manage a breath as her gaze lowered to his mouth, remembering how wonderful his lips felt against hers.

"She said you charmed the guests," he said.

"Was that wrong?"

He shook his head. "That's what we want. Rossi Hotels go beyond routine for our guests. That's why people come to our resorts. That's why they're going to come to the Grand Haven."

"So I did well?"

He finally smiled. "Are you fishing for a compliment?"

She nodded. "Yes."

"Yes, Ms. Covelli, you did very well."

John rested his arm along the back of the sleigh as Angelina rewarded him with a smile. "Now, enough about business. This is downtime." He leaned back and listened to the silence, broken only by the occasional sound of the sleigh bells. But there was no relaxing. His body was on full alert with her next to him.

"Thank you," she said, "but you didn't have to take me for a ride."

He turned to her. Seeing that silly red ski cap on her head, he grinned. She looked adorable. "I'm doing what I want to do." A shiver went through him when her blue eyes looked up at him so trustingly. He cupped the back of her neck and brought her closer. Then his mouth touched hers fleetingly and pulled back. Their eyes met, hers darkened with desire. Without thinking of consequences, he returned, slanting his mouth over hers in a searing kiss that soon had them both heating up under the blanket.

Angelina groaned as his tongue swept past her lips, reaching deep inside and mating with hers. His hands slipped inside her coat and drew her tight against him. By the time he released her, they were both gasping for air.

"Don't tell me you didn't want that as much as I did."

Her eyes shimmered. "No, I can't."

John wished her words gave him more satisfaction. Where would this passion lead them?

The next day, John left Angelina alone. She stayed busy with Shannon, but found she had plenty of time to think about John Rossi and the kisses they had shared. How the man had complicated her once-simple life! She found herself looking for him all the time. Just a quick glance from a distance had her heart racing again. She had to stop it. Her reaction was probably due to the fact that the lodge was a romantic place, and everyone around them was coupled up. Yes, that was it. Once she returned home things would be back to normal, and she could focus on work.

Every bit of the hotel operation fascinated Angelina, and she absorbed information like a sponge, collecting ideas that could be used for the Grand Haven. With more training, she could make a big contribution to the success of the Haven Springs hotel. If only she could convince John.

After a continental breakfast in the inn's café, the next morning, Angelina took the elevator up to the third floor where she was to meet the housekeeping supervisor, Helen. When she arrived she found the cleaning cart next to the Tuscany Suite—John's suite. The door was ajar, so she took it for granted that John had gone skiing and Helen was inside. She pushed open the door and glanced inside the large apartment.

The individual beauty of each room never ceased to amaze her. The large sitting area of this one was adorned with a huge stone fireplace. The glass sliding door opened out to a balcony and endless views of the mountain.

"Must be nice to live like this," she murmured.

"It is," a husky voice answered.

Angelina swung around to find John standing in the doorway to the master bedroom. She gasped, seeing that she had interrupted either his dressing or undressing. He had on ski pants, but he was minus a shirt or sweater, anything that would cover his gorgeous bare chest. Her gaze followed the sprinkling of black hair that narrowed down into his form-fitted pants.

She swallowed hard and managed to speak. "I'm sorry… I had no idea that anyone was here," she said as intense heat raced through her body to her cheeks. Just concentrate on his face, she told herself, but she couldn't do it. His shoulders and arms were beautifully sculpted, and she had an undeniable urge to touch him.

"I'm running a little late, but I'll be heading for the slopes. Give me a minute."

"I'll wait outside." Her pulse pounded so loudly in her ears that she could barely hear him speak.

"Not necessary. I suspect you've seen a few men without shirts." His knowing smile told her he was enjoying her discomfort. "I mean, since you have brothers."

All Angelina wanted to do was escape, but her feet felt rooted to the floor.

He pulled a thermal shirt over his head, then a black sweater. Watching him dress seemed all too intimate.

"Too bad you want to spend all your time working." John grabbed his nylon jacket and gloves off the bed and walked toward her with a smile. "Sure you don't want to take the morning off and go skiing?"

She would love to go, and found she was even considering it, when they were interrupted by a soft voice calling John's name.

They both turned toward the front door of the suite where a small brunette stood. She was also dressed for the slopes.

"Are you ready to go?" she asked John. She gave Angelina a once-over, and then a dismissive look.

"In a minute." John turned back to Angelina. "You sure you don't want to go?" he asked.

"No, I think it would be better if I worked this morning."

He nodded, and went out the door. It didn't seem as if he was that upset that she couldn't go.

Confused, Angelina wondered why that bothered her so much.

Late that afternoon, Angelina returned to her suite, exhausted. But it was a good tired—she'd accomplished a lot with Shannon's help. Right now, all she wanted to do was go to bed, but she knew that sleep would elude her.

As hard as she tried to stay focused on her work, John had managed to invade her head and distract her. He'd made her realize that her life had been empty. She'd been alone since Justin; she had managed, outside family, to keep away from personal relationships. But somehow John had gotten past all the barriers.

Angelina stood, walked to the window and watched the snow fall. She'd been fooling herself when she thought she could come here just for business. She wanted John Rossi, and that terrified her. Angelina shut her eyes, remembering the heated kisses they'd shared. The way he made her feel every time he was near. How his simple touch made her body come alive. A tremor raced through her.

There was a knock on the door. Angelina went to answer it and found Sam holding a long-stemmed red rose.

"This is for you," the young bellman said with a smile, then handed her an envelope. She thanked him and walked back inside.

Knowing the note was from John, Angelina was almost afraid to open it. Finally she tore the envelope and read, "Angelina, have dinner with me tonight in my suite at seven. John."

She could read between the lines. It wasn't just dinner he was asking for. It was much more. And she'd be smart to tear up the note and go to bed and forget all about the invitation.

But since the moment she'd met the man, Angelina hadn't been wise at all. John Rossi was able to get close to her and she couldn't seem to stop it. Worse, she didn't want to. And now, she wasn't thinking sensibly. She held the velvety red rose to her lips. She would go to John's suite and take the *one* night of passion he was offering.

It was seven-fifteen. She wasn't coming, John thought as he went to the table set up by the windows overlooking the mountain. The lights on the slope twinkled in the frigid night air.

As he bent over to blow out the candles, he heard a knock on the door. Suddenly, his heart began pounding erratically. He went to the door and found Angelina standing in the hall.

"Sorry I'm late. I...couldn't decide..."

He took her hand and drew her inside. "I'm glad you came. I wanted so much to spend this evening with you."

Her gaze danced around the room. He could see the panic in her. "Look, Angelina, you can stop acting as if I'm going to pounce on you. I've told you from the beginning that nothing is going to happen unless you want it to."

Her blue eyes met his. "That's what I'm afraid of. I can't seem to stay away from you. I know that I'm not the type of woman you're used to, and I have no idea why you want me."

He cupped her face. "I can give you about fifty reasons. One look from those eyes of yours and you turn me inside out." He drew another shuddering breath. "I can't think of anything but having you in my arms, kissing you until you can't think."

She swallowed. "John...I'm not very good at this. But I want—"

His mouth closed over hers. The kiss was anything but gentle. It was hungry and needy and John wanted her to know the rules from the beginning. He broke off the kiss. ''If you're going to leave, *cara,* you'd better do it now.''

When she didn't budge, he kissed her again, then picked her up in his arms and carried her into his bedroom. ''I want you, Angelina. So much I can't think of anything else.''

''I want you, too.'' she whispered, her arms locked around his neck. He released her and she stood next to the bed. He lowered his head and kissed her cheek softly, then gave his attention to her eyes, her nose, finally her mouth. Light lingering touches that caused her to whimper. He got the message and deepened the kiss. His tongue swept inside, mating hungrily with hers. She clutched his shoulders as he reveled in the feel of her body against his. He moved from her lips and began sampling her tempting neck.

He raised his head. ''We may only have a short time together, but I want to make it perfect for you,'' he said, then he found his way back to her seductive mouth.

Angelina refused to listen to her common sense. All she heard was the drumming of her heart mixed with the sound of soft music playing on the stereo. She wanted tonight. A memory of something she would never have again. She wasn't fooling herself that John was going to confess his undying love for her, nor did she want him to. She wanted one night to forget the loneliness, to pretend she could have something special with a man.

When he broke off the kiss, she whimpered. He smiled, tugged the sweater over her head, tossing it away unnoticed. She trembled when his hands went to unfasten her slacks and soon they were sliding to the floor. Her nervousness grew as she stepped out of them, leaving her standing there in a lacy black bra and matching panties.

John was feasting his eyes on her body as if she were his next meal. "Oh, *cara.* You're so *beautiful.*"

She gathered her courage and stepped forward. "Show me, John." She went to work on his clothes. Her touch was shaky, but she managed to remove his sweater. "Make love to me."

He stripped back the comforter, then placed her down on the cool ivory sheets. "I want you, Angelina. More than you'll ever know."

The only illumination was the moonlight through the window filtering across the big bed. He reached down and unfastened the clasp to her bra, freeing her breasts. His hands took over and began to drive her wild.

Angelina couldn't stop trembling. She wanted so much to please John. Reaching out, she began to stroke his chest, feeling his hot skin against her hands, the sudden power she discovered to make his breath catch as her fingers grazed the nipple all but hidden in the swirl of dark hair. He leaned next to her ear and murmured loving endearments in Italian, causing another warm shiver to run down her spine.

"My turn," he whispered as he slipped silently down beside her in the bed. He bent his head and his mouth covered one breast and sucked gently. Her fingers gripped the sheets as his tongue flicked over the sensitive nipple, making the tip taut, nearly sending her into orbit.

Then guilt overtook her. No matter how much she wanted John, she had no right to feel these things.

John sensed her holding back, tensing up. ''Easy, *cara.* This isn't a race. We'll take this slow,'' he whispered.

She nodded, then pushed against him. ''Make love to me…now.''

''I plan to,'' he promised as his hand went to her belly and slid lower to the edge of her panties. She tensed again then finally pushed away from him.

Reaching for the sheet, she covered her nakedness. ''I'm sorry,'' she breathed, panic laced through her words. ''I thought I could….'' She shook her head. ''But, I can't….''

John pulled her into his arms. ''Shh. I told you we would only go as far as you wanted to go.''

She raised her head, tears filled her eyes. ''You don't understand…. I want to so much. But I would be betraying…''

Before she could explain, there was a soft knock on the door.

''Damn, I forgot about dinner.'' John released her, got up and slipped on his sweater. ''Don't go anywhere,'' he ordered. ''I'll be back.''

Angelina jumped out of the bed, fighting back the tears. More angry at herself than sad at what she'd almost done. Was she crazy? She quickly put on her bra, despite her shaking hands. Next came her slacks and sweater. She wanted desperately to be dressed when she explained that she'd had a moment of insanity.

After slipping on her shoes, she looked up and saw John.

He looked angry.

"How were you planning on sneaking out? There isn't a back door."

"I planned to walk out the front door."

"Think again," he said. "You're not leaving here until you tell me what was going on a few minutes ago."

Angelina didn't want to go into this. "I'd rather not talk about it." She tried to walk past him and he grabbed her.

"Not before you tell me who you think you're betraying."

She looked away. "Can't I just say I changed my mind and leave it at that?"

"I don't think you changed your mind. Something else made you..." His grip tightened. "Who is he? I draw the line at being a substitute for another man. Now, who is he?"

The burning wood in the fireplace crackled. "Justin. We were to be married."

John tensed, then dropped her hand. "Get out." He turned away, realizing she had been using him all along.

She came up behind him. "It's not what you think, John. I was to marry Justin."

John swung around. "Is it my problem that the guy walked out on you?"

A tear escaped and she brushed it away. Damn it. John hated tears. He hated women who used them for their own purposes.

"He didn't walk out. Justin died. We were going to be married, and we never got to make love... I'm sorry." She turned and started for the door.

Ah, hell. He felt like he'd been kicked in the gut.

He went after her. "Angelina, don't leave." He reached for her, but she fought him.

"Stop it, I just want to apologize," he said. "I didn't know."

She nodded. Somehow he managed to guide her to the sofa. He sat down and pulled her onto his lap. He brought her head to his chest and he held her for a long time. She fit so perfectly.

She raised her head. "I'm sorry, I shouldn't have come here."

"Then why did you?" he said.

Her eyes went wide. "Because just once, I wanted to experience a night of passion...a beautiful night I could hold in my memory forever."

John's body began churning once again as memories of what nearly happened in the bedroom flashed back. He wanted nothing more that to show her all about passion. But the realization struck him—Angelina Covelli wasn't a one-night stand.

The next morning, Angelina was waiting by the front entrance with her suitcases. Last night, she had nearly made a terrible mistake, but John had been there for her, holding her, taking her back to her suite where he'd given her the most tender kiss. She'd tried to apologize again, but he'd stopped her, then informed her they would be leaving the next day and to be ready by eight.

John arrived downstairs as Todd drove up. There was more snow due, and he wanted to be out of the area before they got stuck there. No matter how hard he tried, he couldn't quit thinking how much he wanted

Angelina. He had to end the charade and tell her the truth.

The ride into Connecticut was nearly silent, and he welcomed it. He didn't want to analyze what he was feeling. They loaded their things on the plane and Angelina took her seat. John sat down beside her.

He spoke with the pilot and discovered there was going to be a ten-minute delay before they could take off. "I have business to take care of in New York, and you are welcome to go with me," he said to Angelina.

She didn't meet his eyes. "It might be better if I fly on home. I've caused you enough trouble."

He took a deep breath. "Look, Angelina, you were no trouble. About last night..."

"Please, I'd rather not talk about it."

"No. I'm not going to let you keep punishing yourself. All you did was call a halt to...things. You had a right to change your mind." It would be best for all concerned if he let her go home, but he couldn't.

She glanced away. "There's a name for a woman like me."

He took her hand. "I'm not calling you any names."

She looked back at him. "Thank you."

"Will you do me a favor and tell me about Justin?"

She shrugged, then seemed to go into her own world. "We met in college my sophomore year. I fell instantly in love, but I think it took him about two weeks. I dogged his steps everywhere on campus, made sure we ran into each other at least three times a day. Finally he confessed that he couldn't live without me and asked me to marry him after graduation.

"The summer before our senior year, Justin got sick. It took the doctors nearly a month to discover he had a rare form of leukemia. They tried everything, but even the bone-marrow transplant didn't work. He died seven months before our wedding day..." Tears glistened on her cheek.

He held tight to her hand. And before they could make love, he added silently. Had that been the only reason Angelina had wanted him? The feeling struck him hard and fast, he didn't want to be a substitute lover.

She looked at him. "I'm sorry for coming to you last night and expecting you to..."

John cursed to himself. "...fill in."

"No!" she cried. "I wasn't thinking about Justin at all." Suddenly she was blushing. "I was thinking about you."

He was thrilled by her words. "Oh, *cara*. I wanted you, too. But you should hold out for love."

She tilted her head. "You don't sound like a man who doesn't believe in long-term relationships."

"Some of us aren't cut out for love." Somehow in the past month, she had made him wish he was.

"I know I'm not. I'm going to concentrate on my career."

"You'll be good at that, too," he said. "You proved it by how hard you worked at the inn."

"I'm grateful for the opportunity to learn the hotel business."

"Well, New York will be different. I want you to see Rossi International headquarters. And after I finish with business, I want to take you out to a show and dinner. Would you please spend a few days and see the sights with me?"

Her smile lit up her face. "I'd like that."

He hadn't realized he'd been holding his breath waiting for her answer, but he had. Damn. He needed to get focused. The last thing he needed was to get in any deeper. But the warning came too late. He was in way over his head.

Worse, his heart was involved.

Chapter Ten

By the time their plane landed, they had made plans for the evening. To save on time, John had the company helicopter waiting to take them to Rossi International's offices. They were soon flying across a field of high rises and a checkerboard of crowded streets. She'd never in her life seen so many people at once. Too soon they landed on top of the Rossi corporate building in midtown Manhattan.

They rode the elevator down two floors and stepped off into a plush reception area with wheat-colored walls and carpeting. The furnishings were done in emerald-green and blue.

A middle-aged woman with short brown hair met them with a smile. "Well, welcome back, John."

"Hello, Donna," he said.

"How was your time off?" Donna asked, eyeing Angelina closely.

"Nice. How are things going here?"

"It's been quiet." She handed him a pile of messages. "I gave all the urgent calls to Mark." Then she turned to Angelina. "You have to be Angelina Covelli. It's nice to get to meet you."

"I'm glad to meet you, too." Angelina shook her hand. "I think we've talked a few times on the phone."

Donna nodded. "Aren't you lucky to be able to spend a few days in town?" She turned to her boss. "I'm sure John will make your stay memorable."

Angelina noticed John seemed impatient. "We'll just be doing some sightseeing," he said as he took Angelina's hand. "Tell Mark I'll be in my office," he said, eyeing Donna closely. "But only for a short time. I have places to go."

Angelina felt a rush as he tugged her arm and they went down the long hall. When they reached a set of double doors, John ushered her inside. He flicked the switch and the lights came on, revealing the beautifully decorated office.

An enormous glass-and-chrome desk sat in front of the large picture window that overlooked the city. One wall consisted of a bookcase that held books and the latest in high-tech computer equipment. The carpeting was a luxurious, deep maroon color, the kind Angelina would have liked to bury her bare feet in. Her gaze raised to the paintings over the sofa. They were probably worth more than Angelina had made in a year. If she had ever wondered about her and John being different, this proved it. A small-town girl would never fit in here.

"How do you like it?" John's voice brought her back to reality.

"It's a far cry from your office at the hotel."

"Believe it or not, I spend more time in small cramped offices than in here." He stood next to her, very close. He reached for her hand and took her to the window overlooking the city. "I do have a great view." His gaze dropped to her mouth. "I guess being CEO has its privileges." He lowered his head and her lips parted automatically. She shut her mind off to anything but wanting John's kiss.

"So you're saying it pays to know the boss?" she teased.

He nodded right before his mouth touched hers. He pulled back, then took a playful nibble before he came back for more. This time in an all-consuming kiss that when he ended it they were both breathless.

"I thought we weren't going to do that anymore?"

"You were too tempting, *cara.*"

Before she said anything else, there was a sharp knock on the door. A man burst in from a connecting office.

Angelina had moved to the front of the desk as the brown-haired, hazel-eyed man entered the room. He was in his twenties.

"So you finally made it back to sign the contracts—" He looked up and stopped, seeing John wasn't alone. "Sorry. I didn't know you had a guest."

John came around the desk and stood next to her. "Mark, I want you to meet Angelina Covelli."

Mark grinned. "Well, this is a pleasure, Angelina."

They shook hands. "Nice to meet you, too, Mark."

Mark exchanged a look with John. "Now, I can understand why we haven't been able to get you back here." He held up the file in his hands. "But these contracts need to be discussed and signed today."

"Angelina, would you mind? I need to finish up some business matters with Mark."

"Not at all," she said. "I'll go out to the reception area."

"I have a better idea." He smiled then pushed the intercom. A moment later his secretary came through the door. "Donna, could you show Angelina around the office?"

"I'd love to," she said.

Donna took Angelina into her office and answered some questions about Rossi International, but Angelina found that Donna was more interested in asking *her* questions about her family and life in Haven Springs. John arrived after about thirty minutes and took Angelina on the tour of the company. She was totally fascinated with everything, and John took the time to answer all her questions. They even had lunch with Donna and Mark.

Nearly two hours later, they rode the elevator down to the parking garage where the attendant drove up in a shiny black BMW. John opened the passenger-side door for Angelina, before hurrying around the sports car and climbing in. The gray interior smelled of new leather and the dashboard had as many instruments as she imagined it took to fly a plane.

"Nice car," she said, suddenly filled with excitement.

"Thanks." He smiled as he shifted into gear and drove off.

The traffic was slow, but he explained that that was part of New York, along with Broadway, Fifth Avenue, Times Square and the Yankees. Thirty minutes later they had made it to his apartment.

She hadn't thought anything else could surprise her until they arrived at the brick warehouse in the SoHo district. The building had been recently restored and converted into apartments. John parked in the garage on the bottom floor and was greeted by a doorman. They rode to the fifth floor in a modernized freight elevator. Angelina was quickly falling in love with the place. John living here seemed so cosmopolitan...and normal.

"What do you do, just buy up everything you like?" she said half-jokingly.

"Hardly. But this apartment was a good investment, and I wanted a place to live away from my work. Here, I can be myself. Put on my old sweats and take an early-morning run."

The elevator stopped on the top floor. They stepped out into a large hall and John guided her to a set of double oak doors. He inserted a key, then opened the door and stepped inside the dark room.

Soon, light illuminated the spacious living room. It was painted a rich cornsilk color accented by dark-stained woodwork, and had colorful paintings on the walls. The hardwood floor was polished to a high gloss with area rugs scattered around. A row of windows were bare of any drapes, allowing a view of the twinkling night lights of the city.

An overstuffed hunter-green-colored sofa and two print wingback chairs were arranged around a large coffee table. Against the main dividing wall stood a used-brick fireplace. On one side of the hearth was an antique secretary, and on the other side an exquisite ornate grandfather clock with a Roman-numeral face.

"Oh, John, it's beautiful," she breathed as she wandered into the dining room where she found a long mahogany table and six high-back chairs with padded crimson seats. A tall hutch with glass doors displayed fine china and delicate crystal.

"The clock belonged to my parents. Nonna Lia kept it for me."

"Well, it fits in here perfectly."

She moved into another area. The kitchen. Open and airy, the whitewashed cabinets were framed nicely by the almond-tiled counters. A round table with two chairs made a cozy place for two people to share a quiet meal.

"Whoever designed this place did a wonderful job."

"I did most everything myself," he said proudly. "What's done, that is. I took a lot of architecture classes in college. I have more space at the end of the hall where I plan to add a study, and another bedroom. I'm using the area as a gym now."

There was a knock on the door. John opened it to allow the doorman in with their luggage.

John had him wait at the door and walked back to Angelina. "I'm sorry. I'm taking for granted that you'll be staying here in my guest room." He gave her a sheepish look. "But if you like I'll take you to a hotel or the Rossi penthouse."

A warmth spread through her, remembering last night, when they'd nearly made love. The kiss in his office. Too bad she hadn't learned her lesson. "You sure you don't mind having me around?"

He smiled at her. "*Cara,* I wouldn't have asked you to stay, if I didn't want you here."

"Then, I'll stay," she said. "And thank you for taking the time to show me New York."

"My pleasure." He directed the doorman to the guest room, then escorted Angelina inside the large room done in beige tones. A queen-size bed was adorned with a teal-blue comforter and numerous toss pillows. An oak dresser held a photo of an older man she assumed to be his grandfather.

"I hope you'll be comfortable. This is where my grandfather stays when he visits. If not, you can have my room," he said, then rushed on to say, "and I'll sleep here."

Angelina stared at him for a long time without saying anything. Her gaze searched his handsome face. She was getting too used to having him close—and liking it too much. "This room is perfect."

"Good." His dark eyes were dilated, and she could see tiny flecks of gold. "I wouldn't want you to be…uncomfortable."

"I'm fine." Which was a lie. She'd been unbalanced around the man since she'd met him. "I feel like I'm keeping you from work, or something."

"You are, but I decided I deserve the time off." He smiled. "How about we get in a little sightseeing this afternoon?"

"Great, just give me a few minutes to freshen up."

He nodded and stepped outside, closing the door behind him.

Angelina released a long breath and sank down on the bed. How was she going to last two days, living in the same apartment with him? All she could think about was the unbelievable feeling when he touched her, or when his arms held her.

But sooner or later it was all going to end. She'd be back in Indiana, and John Rossi would stay here.

Loaded down with shopping bags, John had no idea how many miles they'd walked, or how many stores Angelina had dragged him into, but she was having fun doing some Christmas shopping. He wanted her to have a good time in New York. And best of all they were out of the apartment and away from temptation. Tonight, he'd planned a quiet dinner and an early evening. He'd have a messenger send over cost sheets for him to look over. That should keep him from thinking about the beautiful woman asleep across the hall.

For tomorrow night, Donna had gotten tickets for a Broadway show and late dinner reservation at his favorite restaurant. By the time they returned to the apartment he hoped he'd be too exhausted to think about how much he wanted her.

Hell, any man would have to have ice in his veins not to want Angelina. Maybe it had been a bad idea to bring her along to New York. He could have easily sent her on to Indiana, but for some reason he needed to clear his conscience and tell her who he was. He was running out of time, but worse, no matter how he sugarcoated the words, he was going to hurt her.

Angelina went up to another shop window. "Oh, John, look at that sweater," she said as she glanced over her shoulder at him. She wore the familiar red knit cap over her long dark hair. "That blue would look perfect on Shelby."

"Yeah, it would be nice."

"Oh, gosh, I forgot. Shelby's pregnant."

"Pregnant?" John murmured, suddenly coming to attention. "They've only been married a few months."

"I know, but Shelby was raised in foster homes. She and Rafe wanted a family from the start."

A peculiar feeling swept over John as he suddenly pictured Angelina with a rounded belly. Pregnant with child. *His* child.

"Isn't it wonderful?" Her voice sounded dreamy.

Had she given up on dreams when Justin died? Had

they planned on a family? Of course, what man wouldn't want Angelina as the mother of his children? A sudden feeling erupted in his gut. He wished he could be the man to give her her dreams.

That night they shared a quiet dinner that had been delivered from the local deli. By nine o'clock, Angelina was nearly falling asleep over her food.

"I think it's time you turned in," John said.

She tried to smile. "I'm sorry I'm such bad company."

"You've had a busy week." He got up and went around the table to help her up. "You just need a good night's sleep. Remember there's the show tomorrow night."

They started down the hall. "I should help you clean up."

He managed to get her to her bedroom door. "You need to be in bed. I'll do it."

She looked up at him, her blue eyes clear and questioning. Holding himself in check, he bent down and kissed her on the cheek, then gently pushed her inside. "Sleep well, *cara,*" he whispered and closed the door. But he couldn't shut out the thought of the desirable woman in the bed only a few feet away.

The next evening, John was dressed in his black suit waiting for Angelina to finish getting ready for the theater. He paced the living room, knowing tonight he had to find a way to tell her everything. Tell her who he was. Who his grandfather was. The thought ate away at his gut like acid. Damn. He never should have let it go this far. If he'd told the Covellis who he was from the start, he wouldn't be in this situation now.

He heard the bedroom door open and he looked up. The air caught in his lungs as he watched Angelina walk toward him. She was dressed in a short black evening dress that caressed her curves just enough to be enticing. Her black high heels made her seem considerably taller and, if possible, made her legs shapelier. Her silky hair was pulled up off her neck by two sparkling clips and small diamonds adorned her ears.

"Do I look okay?" she asked timidly. "The salesclerk said this dress would be all right for tonight."

"You're perfect," he said as he placed her wool jacket across her shoulders, knowing she was far too tempting for them to hang around here. "Let's go."

They arrived at the theater in plenty of time. But Angelina hadn't noticed; she was too fascinated by all the excitement of being at the Broadway play *Les Misérables.*

Afterwards they took a cab to an out-of-the-way restaurant not far from the theater. They shared a quiet intimate meal without much conversation. But every time John glanced across the table at Angelina, he knew that he was falling deeper and deeper.... And it scared the hell out of him.

How could he have let it happen? He'd been so careful to keep an emotional distance. Not to get involved. But it had happened anyway.

"John, are you okay?"

His gaze met hers. "I'm fine. Maybe a little tired."

She smiled and picked up her wineglass. "We have been busy. Today was an unbelievable day. Thank you."

"You're welcome." He reached across the table and took her hand, knowing that it was getting harder and harder to let her go, but he had no choice. "You'll be heading home tomorrow."

She nodded, and he felt her hand tremble. "I feel like I've been gone forever." Her gaze went to his. "I can't thank you enough for this trip. I've learned so much."

"I'll miss you," he said, not caring that the words had slipped out.

She nodded. "I'll miss you, too. But, I guess we both always knew that your life is here...and mine's in Indiana."

He watched the tears well in her eyes. Damn it, how did she manage to reach inside and get a grip on his heart? Suddenly he didn't want to spend the rest of their time together in a crowded restaurant.

He waved for the waiter to bring the check, and within ten minutes they were in a cab heading back to SoHo. They rode back in silence. John was careful to keep his distance. Once he touched her, he wouldn't be able to stop.

And tonight he had to tell her the truth.

John opened the apartment door and Angelina walked inside ahead of him. Unable to resist her, he leaned back on the door and pulled her against him, loving the feeling of her shapely body. They fit together perfectly. Oh, how he wanted her.... No! With the last of his strength, he managed to release her.

"Angelina, we have to talk." Needing space, he went into the living room. He pushed a few buttons on the CD player, and the voice of the Italian opera singer, Andrea Bocelli, filled the room with a romantic ballad. Big mistake. But before he could correct it, Angelina came up to him.

She returned to his arms. ''What do you want to talk about, John?'' she whispered. ''How I realize that I have feelings for you? I tried to push you away, but can't anymore. I don't want to go back to Indiana without you knowing how I feel.''

Instantly fire flamed inside him, making him forget all reason. He took her mouth in another hungry kiss. Hot sensations raced through him, but he suddenly came to his senses. He gripped her arms and pulled back.

''Wait, Angelina. We need to talk first. There are things that you need to know.''

''What things? That you don't believe in permanent relationships? That doesn't matter. I care about you, John. I think you care about me.''

''I do, damn it.'' He moved away again. One more touch and he was a goner. ''That's why you have to listen to me.''

She stopped and looked up at him, her face so full of trust. ''If you're trying to let me down…''

He swung her into his arms, sliding an arm around her waist before she could gauge his intent. She gasped as his mouth came down on hers in an intimate, searing kiss that demanded a response. And she did respond, with a passion that matched his own. When he finally raised his head she was clinging to him, just as he wanted her to.

He walked across the room as he worked on calming his breathing. ''I think I've proven my point that I'm not trying to let you down. Now stay over there until I say what I have to say.''

She nodded as the music surrounded them, blanketing them in intimacy. Besides a small lamp, the only other light was moonlight streaming through the window.

"When the Grand Haven Hotel came up for sale last year, I'd never heard of Haven Springs, Indiana. I did some research and discovered that the area could handle a Rossi hotel. So Mark and I began to look into purchasing the property and researching companies to handle the renovations." He paused to take a breath. "Then I got the list of contractors and saw the Covelli name on it...." He glanced at her. "I recognized the name, and I did some more investigating to see if your family was the same Covellis I knew of. I've told you my grandfather was from Italy. And he still lives there."

Angelina nodded.

"Well, what I didn't tell you was that he came from Tuscany. His family has owned a vineyard there for generations. He knows your Nonna Vittoria."

"Really? She'll be delighted to hear you know someone from her village. Who is your grandfather?"

John drew a breath. "Giovanni Valente."

The excitement died from her eyes as she shook her head. "No, that can't be. Giovanni Valente cursed our family."

"It's true, Angelina. But what happened fifty years ago shouldn't matter to us."

"If it doesn't, why didn't you tell me in the beginning? Why did you lie?"

"I never lied. I was curious to meet the family that caused my grandparents so much heartache."

She gasped. "The Covellis caused the Valentes heartache? I believe we were the ones who were cursed. Why did you hire us? To amuse yourself?"

"One thing has nothing to do with the other. I gave

your brothers the hotel job because they were the best qualified."

"We don't need charity. You lied to us all along."

"I did no such thing," he denied. "I was only doing my job. Now looking back, I should have told you...." He wanted to go to her, to hold her. To make things right again.

Without a sound, she turned to leave.

Panic raced through him, realizing how much he wanted her to stay. "Please don't go."

She glanced over her shoulder. "You've had your laugh, now leave me a little dignity."

"I'm not laughing." He took her arm and turned her around. "I care about you, Angelina."

The buzz of the intercom startled them, and John went to answer it. The doorman informed him that his grandfather was downstairs waiting in the lobby. What unbelievable timing! Giovanni wasn't supposed to arrive until next week. John said that he'd be down in a moment.

"Look, Angelina. I have to go downstairs for a minute. Please, just wait until I get back, we have to talk this out."

She folded her arms and refused to answer him.

John raced out the door and down the elevator. He didn't need this tonight. He didn't need this ever. Somehow he had to stop this woman from walking away.

The door opened and he rushed out to find his grandfather. They hugged and exchanged greetings in Italian.

"Why didn't you tell me you were coming early?"

"I didn't know until I spoke with Signora Donna, yesterday," Giovanni said. "She told me you had returned from Vermont and came into the office with a beautiful young woman. Her name was Angelina Covelli. This Angelina is related to Vittoria, *sì?*"

John nodded. "*Sì,* Nonno. She's Vittoria's granddaughter. And I think I'm in love with her."

Angelina fought her tears as she changed into slacks and a sweater. Then she began tossing her clothes into her suitcases and planning her escape. But, by the time she made it to the front door, John was there with a white-haired man.

In his late sixties or seventies, he was tall and broad-shouldered. His gaze met hers and he froze, complete surprise on his face. Finally he turned to John and spoke in Italian.

"Angelina, this is my grandfather, Giovanni Valente."

"*Ciao,* Signorina Angelina," Giovanni said with a smile. "You are as *bella* as Vittoria."

"Signore Valente, I'm sorry, but I can't talk about this."

John interrupted. "My grandfather had no idea that I knew the Covellis," he said. "So don't be angry with him."

"No!" Giovanni said. "This is all my fault. It was my mother who cursed your *famiglia,* Angelina. John wasn't even born. Be angry with me."

Angelina wanted to disappear. "I'm not angry with anyone. I just want to go home." She started for the door.

John grabbed her arm to stop her. "Please, Angelina, don't go like this. I care about you."

She pulled away from his touch. "If you care anything about me or my family, you'll leave us alone for another fifty years." She walked out and slammed the door behind her. The sound echoed in the silent room.

A dull pain constricted John's chest, making it hard to breathe. The scene was familiar, another person he cared about leaving him. His shoulders slumped, he was suddenly tired. He looked at his grandfather.

"I'm sorry, I couldn't help," Giovanni said.

John went to the window, all at once feeling empty. Angelina could have filled that emptiness. "Why can't we have the women we love?" he murmured.

Giovanni came to his grandson and put a hand on John's shoulder. "Sometimes we look for the wrong woman. I realize now that Vittoria wasn't for me to have. She loved another man long before I asked her to marry me. But my *stupido* pride couldn't let her go. Then for years I hung on until my bitterness even drove my Lia away. Even my own daughter was injured by my loveless marriage and passed that hurt on to you." He looked John in the eyes. "I'm sorry. *Our* family has been cursed because I wouldn't let myself love. You can change that, *figlio.* Let Angelina show you how. Let her love you."

But Angelina was gone. Love was gone. "Doesn't matter anymore. You heard her. It's hopeless, just like you and Vittoria."

Giovanni smiled sadly. "No, no, son. You can't think that. Besides, there's a big difference. Vittoria loved another man, Enrico. Your Angelina loves you. And if she is anything like her grandmother, there is only room in her heart for one man." The older man reached into his jacket pocket, pulled out a velvet box and opened the lid. The beautiful ruby and diamond ring sparkled inside. The bride's ring. The ring that Giovanni was to slip on Vittoria's finger so long ago.

But that had not been meant to be. In anger, Giovanni had cursed the Covellis and stolen the bride's ring. Now, it was past time to return it. To end the curse that plagued both families for years.

John swallowed, wanting to hope, but afraid to. So many times love had eluded him. "I don't believe in love." It hurts too much, he added silently.

"Fine, be stubborn. Look where it's gotten me. Nowhere. I can look forward to being alone for the rest of my life." Giovanni looked out at the twinkling lights of the city. "I guess it won't bother you when Angelina finds another man. A man who will love her. A man who will share her life. Her dreams."

The pain of Giovanni's words nearly choked John. "Stop it," he cried. "Okay, I get your point."

"Then do something." The old man held up the ring. "The curse ends when our two families get together."

"She doesn't want anything to do with me."

"I bet you can change her mind. Do you think that Angelina would have been so angry if she didn't care? The tears in her *bella* blue eyes were for the man she loves."

John's heart raced with hope. He took the velvet box from his grandfather. "I'm going to need this. Come on, I have to convince one beautiful woman that I love her."

Chapter Eleven

The next afternoon, Angelina sat up in her bed and checked the clock on the nightstand. It was already after one o'clock. She should have been up by now, but knowing she would have to face more questions from the family had kept her isolated in her room.

She had wasted enough tears on John during the red-eye flight, not to mention sobbing all the way home after Rafe had picked her up at the airport.

How could she have let herself fall…? No, she wasn't going to think about him anymore. If she'd had any feelings for the man, he'd killed them. Anger was the only emotion she felt when she thought of John Rossi and his deception.

Now she had to pull herself together and go on. Right. How was she supposed to work for Rossi International knowing John had lied to her and her family? Tony had informed her that the contract with Rossi International was ironclad. No way out. Maybe the contract was ironclad, but her job wasn't. She could resign from the project, leave town and forget about John. Forget how easily she'd fallen for his charms—how she had nearly made love to the man. Fresh anguish filled her heart. Had she betrayed Justin's memory?

There was a soft knock on the door, and her grandmother peeked inside. "Good afternoon, Lina."

Angelina watched as Nonna Vittoria walked forward carrying a tray of food.

"You need to eat," she said. "You will feel better."

"Thank you, Nonna, but I'm not really hungry."

Nonna set the tray on the table next to the bed. "That usually happens when you're in love."

Angelina sighed. "I'm not in love," she denied as her gaze met her grandmother's wise, caring dark eyes. Angelina's lips began to quiver. "He lied to me, Nonna."

"Was it really a lie?" Vittoria reached out and stroked her cheek. "Don't blame John for something that happened over fifty years ago. Neither of you children were responsible for what Giovanni or I did."

"It was the Valente family who caused the trouble. You only wanted to marry the man you loved. Nonno Enrico."

"And when we're in love, we don't always think with our heads. Maybe John did the same. Maybe he was curious at first, maybe even a little jealous of what the Covelli family had. Then he grew to care about you. Didn't he finally tell you the truth, even though he feared he would lose you?"

Angelina didn't want to hear this. "There was nothing to lose. I...we weren't involved," she said, knowing it was partly a lie. "I mean, I love Justin. I'll never love another man like I loved him."

"Of course you won't," Nonna said. "Each love is different." Her aged hand took her granddaughter's. "And you have been blessed to know love once before. Some people, maybe John, have never known what it is like to love someone. Maybe he wanted to take a chance with you, but was afraid. I don't think that Justin would expect you to go through life closing yourself off from happiness."

A tear rolled down Angelina's cheek. Vittoria went on. "I believe you are so angry because you have feelings for John Rossi. Feelings that scare you, so you're ready to walk away just to protect your heart."

Angelina tried to deny it, but she couldn't find the words.

"And what of John?" Vittoria continued. "Seems his life has been pretty lonely. He works all the time, traveling around the world. You told me his parents died when he was just a boy. And Giovanni helped raise him, no doubt teaching his grandson the bitterness he'd felt toward the Covellis." Vittoria's gaze met hers. "And yet when John discovered that the Covellis who bid on the hotel job were one and the same family that had made his grandfather's life miserable, didn't he still give Rafe and Rick the job?"

Angelina's defenses were weakening. "That was business."

"I believe that there were plenty of companies in Louisville who would have loved to have the job. But John gave it to the Covellis. Do you know how hard that must have been for him? That's like a betrayal to the Valente family. Now, why do you suppose he did that?"

Angelina didn't want to hope there was a more personal reason. "What about the curse?"

Vittoria stood. ''Oh my, Lina. Has our family really been cursed? Just look around you. There may have been struggles along the way, but we've all been blessed with our big, happy family. You've had the love of a wonderful man. Now you have another chance at happiness. Some people aren't that lucky, and some, like John, don't trust love enough to reach out for it.

John *had* reached out—to her. But she had turned away. Oh, God, how could she have done that? Panic raced through her. Had he cared about her? Maybe even loved her? She had to find him. ''Oh, Nonna, I've been so terrible to John. I have to go to New York.'' She got out of bed. ''I have to see him.'' She went to her closet and pulled out gray wool slacks and a pink sweater. ''Can you call the airport and see if I can get a plane?''

Vittoria smiled. ''I don't think you need to go to New York.'' She reached in her pocket and pulled out a paper. ''John called this morning. He wants to see you.''

Angelina's eyes widened. ''He's in town? Where?'' She read his note. ''Please, Angelina, I need to see you. Come to the hotel at your convenience. John.''

Her hopes faded at the word *convenience*. He didn't seem anxious to see her. And why should he? She had basically told him to get lost. Why had it taken so long for her to realize she loved him?

''He wants to see you.''

''I know, Nonna. I'll go, but I doubt John wants any more than to talk to his project manager.''

Thirty minutes later, Angelina arrived at the hotel, only to find the place empty. No workmen around and her brothers weren't to be found. Harry wasn't even at the door. Suddenly it felt like the first day she'd arrived for the job. She'd had so many hopes that day. She was going to take on the world, or at least Rossi International's CEO. Find independence, make a career for herself. None of that mattered now. She had lost what she really wanted...John.

Her heart raced as she walked through the lobby. No changes downstairs, yet. Her brothers had been concentrating their efforts on the balcony. She started up the stairs, finding herself reluctant to make the journey. All her joy for the project had disappeared. Taking hold of the brass railing, she began her climb to the top when something caught her attention. She turned and caught sight of a figure standing in the shadows.

Her breathing stopped when she recognized John. He was dressed as he had been the first day she'd come to see him, in jeans, a denim shirt and work boots.

"So you finally decided to come by," he said as he walked toward her.

A deep yearning centered in her chest and all she could do was stare at the handsome man. Had it been less than twenty-four hours since she'd seen him? "I thought your note said at my convenience." A little shaky, she started down the steps.

"No, stay where you are. I have something to say, and when you're close, I can't think straight."

She felt the same way. She nodded as his dark gaze caught hers with a mesmerizing look.

John tried to slow his breathing as he made his way to the bottom of the steps. "Angelina, I know you are angry with me, and you have every right to be. I should have told you who I was from the beginning. But as I've explained to your family—"

"You talked with my family?" she interrupted.

He nodded. "Yes, when I got into town I called the house. Your brothers wouldn't let me talk to you, so I asked them to meet me here this morning. My grandfather came back with me."

"Oh, no. Nonna Vittoria..."

He raised a calming hand. "No, it's okay. They've spent some time together, too. Talking about the past."

She blinked her eyes, looking hurt. "It seems that everyone is talking but me."

He took another step. "Believe me, *cara.* You were the only one I came to see, but I knew that your brothers would never let me near you without knowing my intentions."

"Intentions?"

He found his legs were shaky, but he couldn't back down now. She was everything he'd ever wanted, and somehow he had to make her believe that. "I never meant to hurt you. I said in New York, at first I was curious about the Covellis. And later, I was jealous, because you had so much. So much family, so much love." He looked away. "God, this is hard."

"Please, don't stop," she begged.

Her clear blue eyes drew him back, giving him courage.

"I was attracted to you from the first time I saw you standing right here on these steps. When I discovered who you were, I knew I was in trouble. I tried to fight the attraction, but you managed to get into my head, you interrupted my work, you even appeared in my dreams. Finally the night of the party, when I kissed you, I knew I had to have you in my life." His gaze stayed locked with hers. "Then you told me that you didn't want a relationship with me, you only wanted a job at Rossi International."

She tried to speak, but he held up his hand to stop her.

"I was hurt. I had a serious relationship once. I gave my heart only to discover later that she only wanted me for what I could give her monetarily. I wasn't going to let that happen again. I only took you to Vermont to seduce you. I was going to use you, like you were trying to use me."

Angelina saw the pain and loneliness on his face. "Why didn't you?"

"I found I didn't want to be a substitute for another man. And I was jealous of what I couldn't have. You." He managed a nervous smile. "It's kind of ironic. I finally found someone who I was willing to risk my heart for, but you cared for another man. And when you discovered who I was, you'd end up hating me."

"So why risk it?" She knew how hard this was for him.

"I couldn't give you up. I wanted you more than any woman I'd known." He rubbed his forehead. "And when we arrived in New York, my hopes were raised, I saw that you were starting to care for me, too. You wanted *me* last night, *cara.* I saw it in your eyes."

"Yes, I wanted you." She was trembling. "And you could have made love to me. Why didn't you?"

John drew a long breath. "Because I want more than your body. I want all of you.... I want your love."

Angelina was afraid to move, to speak. Finally she forced out the words, "You love me?" Fresh tears formed in her eyes as he nodded.

He climbed the steps until he reached her. "Please,

don't cry,'' he said. ''I didn't say it to make you unhappy.''

She shook her head. ''I'm not unhappy. Oh, John.''

''Don't tell me Justin is the only man in your life. I'm going to make you change your mind.'' He took her hand. ''You've got to give me a chance. There is magic between us.''

She nodded. ''There is, isn't there.''

''Then surely there can be room in your life…''

''But you live in New York. I can't fit in.''

He smiled. ''Then I can come work from here. I like Haven Springs—a lot.'' His expression turned serious. ''Tell me, Angelina, is there a chance for us? Could you love me?''

''Oh, John….'' She went into his arms. ''I tried so hard to fight my feelings for you.''

''Don't…'' His mouth closed over hers smothering any more of her words. She groaned as his arms slipped around her back, pulling her against him so he could feel the warmth of her luscious body. He gathered his control and released her.

Seeing the desire flashing in her blue eyes, and her mouth swollen from his kisses, John wanted desperately to carry her off somewhere to finish what they'd started in Vermont, convince her they were meant to be together. ''Oh, *cara,* I love you so much. I want to marry you.''

She gasped.

''I'm sorry, I didn't mean to blurt it out like that.''

''It's fine,'' she said as a pretty blush colored her cheeks. ''But would you mind repeating it?''

He took her hands in his and he felt her trembling. ''I said I love you, Angelina Covelli, with all my heart.'' He glanced around at the dim lobby, then down at her. ''I wish the renovations were finished. It seems a little dingy now. But I wanted us to return to the first place I laid eyes on you.''

Angelina felt like she was walking through a dream, but if she were, she didn't want to wake up. ''John, I love you, too.''

''*Dio, cara.* You have no idea how badly I've wanted to hear those words from you,'' he breathed. He searched her face. ''From the moment I met you, I was hooked. Am I forgiven for keeping my background a secret?''

''For every sin you ever committed,'' she whispered, pressing her body against his, aching for him. ''Just kiss me.''

John smiled again just before his mouth slanted over hers, showing her how much he wanted her, and needed her in his life. He wrapped his arms around her and drew her closer. With a deep groan he finally broke away. ''There is one more thing.'' He reached into his jeans pocket and pulled out a ring. Not just any ring, but the ruby bride's ring.

''Oh John, that's...my grandmother's ring. It looks like the groom's ring my grandfather wore.''

He nodded his head. ''Yes, it is. I tried to give it to her this morning but she refused to take it. She said it belongs to the first-born daughter. *You.* What do you say we put an end to this curse?''

Then, as if John couldn't shock her anymore, he went down on one knee and looked up at her with an expression of love that Angelina would remember all her life.

''Angelina, will you do me the honor of marrying me?''

She could see the love in his eyes, just as she could feel it in her own heart. "Oh, yes, I'll marry you."

He took her trembling hand and managed to slip the ring on her finger. Then he stood, and took her mouth in a kiss that told her of his love, and promised that he was the man who would love her forever.

"Hey, are you two about finished down there?"

John grinned when they heard Rafe's voice. "I think the family wants to know the outcome of our talk."

Angelina gasped. "They've been up there the whole time?"

"Just as I said, your brothers are very protective."

She laughed. "Think you can handle this family?"

He pulled her against him. "As long as you come along in the package." He kissed her again, then finally released her. "I think we better call everyone down before they think I stole you away. Besides, we've got to plan a wedding."

"You can come out now," he called up to the balcony.

He held her next to him and they looked up to see her family lined up against the railing.

"She said yes." John yelled, triumphant.

Cheers broke out, and they yelled back congratulations. Surprisingly, Vittoria and Giovanni were standing side by side.

"When's the wedding?" Shelby called to her as she patted her rounded stomach. "If you wait too long Jill and I will be huge."

"Soon," John said.

Angelina looked up at John and they exchanged a glance that she'd seen shared a hundred times between her brothers and their wives. Love. "Soon," she agreed.

He leaned down and whispered in her ear. "I'd like ours to be the first wedding reception at the new Grand Haven," he suggested. "What do you think?"

"Is this another thing you discussed with my family?"

He gave her a sexy smile that had her melting. "I told you I had to tell them my intentions. So what is your answer, *cara?* Shall we have our reception here?"

"I think the hotel won't be finished soon enough. I want to be your wife as soon as possible."

He squeezed her close. "I like your eagerness."

Angelina gasped. "I think you better marry me soon. Until you do, my brothers will be watching your every move."

"Good point," he said. "Guess I'll just have to pay the crew to work overtime to get things done sooner...for my impatient bride."

Angelina looked up at the balcony again and saw Vittoria and Giovanni smiling. This was a new beginning for everyone.

Holding Jill's hand, Rick started down the stairs. "Hey, does this mean that the curse will finally be broken?"

Angelina looked up at her grandmother, then back to her future husband. "Oh, Rick, there was never a curse, really. Look around. The Covellis have always been blessed."

John leaned down and placed a tender kiss on Angelina's lips and said, "We are all blessed now, *cara.* The Covellis and the Valentes. And I never believed that more than I do right now."

Epilogue

February 14th, John and Angelina's wedding day, was perfect.

By noon, Saint Anthony's Catholic Church was filled to capacity with friends and family gathered to wish the bride and groom well and to see that the Covelli curse lifted after so many years.

The rings that had been separated for the past fifty years were carried down the aisle by the ring bearer, two-year-old Lucas Covelli. The priest blessed them and the groom gave the bride's ring to his wife, then the bride gave the groom's ring to her husband.

The fifty-year-old curse ended as the two families were finally united in marriage—in everlasting love.

An hour later, a white limousine pulled up in front of the Grand Haven Hotel and John climbed out in his black tux. He reached back inside and assisted his wife out of the car, careful not to damage the antique-white wedding dress, the same dress that Vittoria had worn on her wedding day.

The beaded bodice was fitted to Angelina's tiny waist. The neckline and sleeves were off the shoulder, revealing her graceful neck, which showed off the gift John had given his new wife, a heart-shaped diamond necklace. The full skirt draped to the floor with a long train trimmed in lace. She wore a beaded headpiece with an elbow-length veil. Her shiny black hair was tucked underneath, pulled up in curls. She took his breath away.

John reached for his wife's hand and they walked up the carpeted entry and into the restored hotel lobby. Angelina paused taking in all the colorful flowers. Roses. Hundreds of roses everywhere. A fountain in the middle of the room spouted champagne for the guests. The new scarlet carpeting was plush beneath their feet as they headed up the wide staircase. They posed for a few pictures, then continued upstairs to the ballroom.

They walked into the grand room with its elegant wine-and-blue wallpaper. The rich new woodworking and refinished floor looked as they had a hundred years ago. The Covellis knew their business well. Rafaele Covelli would have been proud of his family. John wished he could have met the man.

They posed for more pictures, then made their way to the head table and sat down.

Angelina leaned toward John with a big smile. "You seem to be holding up okay. I thought for sure you would have run for the hills."

He took her hand. "As long as you're beside me, I'm fine. Just don't forget we leave for the plane in three hours. I'm looking forward to having you all to myself.''

She kissed him. ''I'm looking forward to that, too.''

He searched her lovely face. ''Have I told you how beautiful you look?''

''Several times. But don't stop.''

''Never,'' he promised. ''I love you, Mrs. Rossi. You've made me whole.''

She touched his face. ''And you gave me the love I never thought I could have. I can't wait until we're alone and I can show you how much I want you.''

He brought her hand to his mouth and kissed her fingertips. ''You sure you want to fly to Vermont tonight?'' he asked.

She nodded. ''You promised we were going to finish what we started. I hope you're a man of your word.''

He groaned. ''I don't know if I can wait that long to make you mine.''

''We've waited this long. I want our special night to be at the inn.''

''I love you. I was blessed from the first moment I laid eyes on you.''

Her blue eyes were shimmering. ''I feel the same way about you. And I'm a little anxious to get out of here, but these family gatherings could last forever.''

John squeezed his wife's hand. ''As long as we last forever.''

Then before she answered, his mouth captured hers in a heated kiss. Desire spread through him as he pulled her close. The wineglasses chimed as the kiss continued, but he barely heard. He held all his dreams in his arms—the family he'd always wanted and the love he never thought possible until Angelina came into his life and showed him how to take the first step.

Three years later, Nonna Vittoria sat in the rocking chair with her great-granddaughter asleep in her arms.

Five-year-old Lucas and his two-and-a-half-year-old sister, Tessa, came into the room. "Tell us a story, Nonna."

She hushed them so they wouldn't wake two-year-old Rafaele III asleep on the floor. "If you sit down and be quiet."

The children did as she asked. Lucas, Tessa, Rafaele III, and six-week-old Lia. Vittoria smiled as she thought back to her younger years. Her childhood in Italy. Her first and only love, Enrico. She had been truly blessed with love and family. And now there was another generation of Covellis. And it all had started with love. An undying love that had kept the family together through good and bad times over the last fifty years. She wouldn't change a thing.

"Tell us about Nonno Enrico," Lucas asked. "About his medals that he got when he flew in the airplane in Italy. And how you saved his life."

Vittoria had told this story a hundred times, but neither she, nor the children ever got tired of hearing it. "His plane crashed near my village. He was hurt, so I hid him in our barn until I could get him to safety."

"Then we all got cursed," the five-year-old blurted out.

"Oh, no." Vittoria shook her head as she eyed

every one of her beautiful great-grandchildren. Emotions clogged her throat. "The Covellis have always been blessed."

* * * * *

WITH THESE RINGS
a romantic miniseries
by Patricia Thayer

Book 1
THE SECRET MILLIONAIRE
Special Edition #1252

Book 2
HER SURPRISE FAMILY
Silhouette Romance #1394

Book 3
THE MAN, THE RING, THE WEDDING
Silhouette Romance #1412